Death on Doomsday

By Elizabeth Lemarchand

Elizabeth Lemarchand

Death on Doomsday

Rupert Hart-Davis   London

Granada Publishing Limited
First published 1971 by Rupert Hart-Davis Ltd
3 Upper James Street London W1R 4BP

ISBN 0 246 64032 4
Printed in Great Britain by Novello Co Ltd
Borough Green Kent

To M.E.P. and O.W.

All places and characters in this story are entirely
the product of the author's imagination.

Tea
room
and
shop

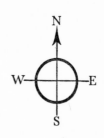

N

W —— E

S

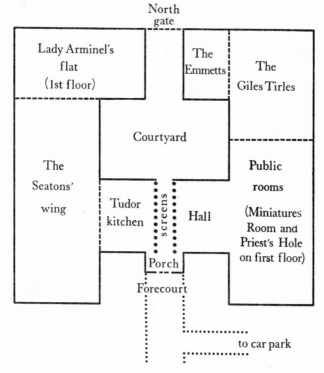

North
gate

Lady Arminel's
flat
(1st floor)

The
Emmetts

The
Giles Tirles

Courtyard

The

Seatons'

wing

Tudor
kitchen

screens

Hall

Public

rooms

(Miniatures
Room and
Priest's Hole
on first floor)

Porch

Forecourt

to car park

BRENT

CHIEF CHARACTERS

THE HOUSE
BRENT, in the county of Midshire, seat of the Tirles since the fifteenth century.

THE FAMILY
Roger, eighth Earl of Seton
Bridget ('Biddy'), Countess of Seton
Lady Caroline Tirle, their elder daughter
The Honourable Giles Tirle, Lord Seton's younger brother
Felicity Tirle, his wife
Robert Tirle, their elder son
Lady Arminel Tirle, half-sister to Lord Seton and Giles Tirle

RETAINERS
Mrs Pringle ('Ping'), ex-nanny to the Setons
Mrs Peggy Blackmore, Lord Seton's secretary
Bill Emmett, handyman-caretaker
Elsie Emmett, his wife
Rosalie Emmett, their daughter, engaged to Dick White

PROFESSIONAL ADVISER on the opening of BRENT to the public, Maurice Corden, of Stately Homes Ltd

A CONSULTANT ENGINEER
George Snell, A.M.I.C.E.

THE POLICE
Inspector Diplock of the Midshire constabulary
Detective-Superintendent Tom Pollard, Detective-Sergeant Toye, and Detective-Constables Boyce and Strickland of New Scotland Yard

Jane, wife of Detective-Superintendent Pollard
The Pollard twins, Andrew and Rose, aged eight months

CHAPTER ONE

'Lions? Don't be such an ass, Arminel.' The eighth Earl of Seton shot an exasperated glance at his half-sister, six years his senior. 'Opening a place to the public doesn't have to mean turning it into a shambles.'

'Lions . . . shambles . . . horrid suggestions of the Colosseum,' Felicity Tirle remarked *sotto voce* to her husband, Lord Seton's younger brother, who was sitting beside her. 'Definitely not lions, Arminel darling,' she went on aloud. 'Incompatible with the ethos of Brent. So are fun fairs. There'd have to be teas, of course, but the emphasis would be on culture. And horticulture, naturally. That's where you come in.'

'Or where I go out.' Lady Arminel Tirle planted her empty coffee cup on a table with symbolic finality. 'Imagine it. Mobs trampling everywhere, dropping orange peel and picking the flowers. Pinching cuttings too, I expect.'

She spoke with her characteristic vigour, a slight, energetic spinster in her early fifties who had made the market garden on the estate pay. Her short dark hair was barely touched with silver, and an open-air life had weathered her complexion to copper-rose. She had the Tirle high cheekbones and good nose, and was wearing slacks and a polo-neck jersey.

'But it wouldn't be that kind of mob,' Giles Tirle broke in eagerly. 'You may get a cutting swiper anywhere, but without gimmicks we'd only draw the sort of people who care about places like this. I'm all for opening—the sooner the better. Historic houses are part of the nation's cultural heritage.'

He leaned forward as he talked, his eyes bright with enthusiasm behind massive horn-rimmed spectacles. There was a strong family likeness between him and his half-sister, but he had a donnish look, and the pallor of an indoor man. A social historian and an authority on English domestic architecture, he was a Fellow of an Oxford college and confusedly Left in sympathy.

'Coachloads of Conservative women and Mothers' Union,' commented his wife, her intelligent, rather angular face amused. 'Can't you see them arriving, and Blennerhasset's Tours cashing in like mad?'

There was a pause, as Lord Seton lit another cigarette. The clear light of a fine spring afternoon flooded through the mullioned windows, picking out the geometrical pattern of the Elizabethan panelling and the great coat of arms over the fireplace. There was a spurt of flame as a log rolled over on the hearth. He got up to throw another log on the fire, and remained standing, his left hand thrust into his trouser pocket and absently fingering some loose coins. To his secret chagrin he was only vestigially a Tirle in appearance, having inherited the fair colouring and conventional upper-class good looks of his mother's family. More usefully he had inherited the Tirle business acumen, which sometimes lay dormant through an entire generation, and since coming into the title some years earlier in his middle thirties he had nurtured the family finances with marked success. Arminel shared his abilities to a lesser extent, and as he watched her unobtrusively he saw that her initial hostility to the idea of admitting the public to Brent was giving way to a guarded interest.

'Unlike Giles,' he said, expelling a mouthful of smoke, 'I don't feel the slightest obligation to share Brent with the masses. As far as I'm concerned, opening the place is purely a question of money.'

'That's a point of view which I—' Giles began heatedly, but Arminel swept him aside.

'Should we ever do more than break even?' she asked.

Roger Seton concealed his satisfaction and picked up some papers.

'Take Holchester Manor,' he said. 'About our size, with roughly equal attractions and no gimmicks laid on. Old Pomfret-Guille has let me have some figures. They're confidential, of course.'

He proceeded to summarise, with comments, the financial outcome of the opening of Holchester Manor over a period of four years.

'As you can see,' he said, 'we probably shouldn't do more than recover our initial outgoings in the first year, and only break even in the second, but on the other hand, we're much more on the map than Holchester, and with competent publicity we might build up quite quickly. In the long term, I should expect enough to come in at least to keep up the house and grounds to a decent standard. With costs rising the whole time this is going to be a problem without extra income from somewhere.'

'How much private life should we have left?' asked Felicity.

'Not much in the season,' Lord Seton replied frankly. 'Not if we want to make money, that is. It pays to put in an appearance, and wage bills would have to be kept down. We'd have summer afternoon opening only—we aren't in the all-the-year-round category. Biddy is game to organise the cleaning and the flowers, and so on.'

Bridget Seton, lovely and a little withdrawn, raised a Georgian silver coffee-pot, and looked around enquiringly.

'I don't think there'd be any difficulty in getting in extra help,' she said, refilling her sister-in-law's cup. 'Once the village had got used to the idea of the house being opened, they'd want to be in on it. But as I've told Roger, the thought of taking people round just paralyses me. I always muddle the different periods . . . I'm not a bit like Hermione Pomfret-Guille.'

'Thank God you aren't,' her husband replied with feeling. 'Anyway if you take on the cleaning women and the flowers, you certainly shouldn't be called on for showing round. We'd have to recruit a squad of guides locally to help out, of course.'

'Oh, but I shouldn't want to contract out of anything,' she said hastily, an undercurrent of emotion in her voice. 'After all, it's a question of Robert's future here, and his children after him, isn't it?'

A slight constraint was perceptible. Roger Seton turned to throw his cigarette end into the fire, and Giles and Felicity, parents of Robert, shifted their positions on the sofa. Bridget Seton's unconscious masochism was always an embarrassment. She was dominated by a sense of failure in not having produced a male heir to Brent and the title. After the birth of her second daughter, an illness and inevitable operation had put an end to her hopes.

Lady Arminel cleared her throat briskly, and dispelled the tension by deliberately introducing a thorny subject.

'Well,' she remarked, 'if we must go to these lengths to safeguard Brent's future, let's hope Robert won't break his neck out hunting in the meantime.'

Giles and Felicity rose to the implied criticism of their younger son, Paul.

'What none of you seem to realise is that Paul is simply expressing the Zeitgeist of the entire rising generation—the universal challenge to established values at the present time. He's not the only member of the family, either, who's showing signs of—'

'Anyway, he's calming down,' interposed Felicity, deftly cutting off her husband in full cry. 'Why, the present school's kept him for nearly five terms.'

'Well,' said Lord Seton from the hearthrug, ignoring the diversion, 'do I take it that we're agreed to accept a grant from the Historic Buildings people, and open the place to the public?'

There was general assent.

'What's the next step?' enquired Arminel.

He appeared to deliberate.

'I think the best thing would be to get the firm of consultants who advised Pomfret-Guille to send a chap down to have a look round. They'll charge quite a hefty fee, of course, but you can't make money without spending it.'

Lord Seton forebore to mention that he had already paid two visits to the office of the firm in question, and had been expensively lunched on the second occasion.

Ten days later, Maurice Corden of Stately Homes Limited, who had so successfully advised the Pomfret-Guilles on the opening of Holchester Manor to the public, drove down from London to Brent. Drawing up at the main gates he noted approvingly that the house was invitingly visible from the London-Crockmouth road across the park, the Elizabethan E of grey stone admirably sited against a backdrop of wooded hillside. A useful touch of theatre for a start, he thought, and on a rather statelier scale than he'd expected. He gave it a long, hard look, his long nose twitching slightly in interested anticipation, and let in the clutch.

As the park with its clusters of fine trees flowed past on either side the house became progressively more imposing. The car turned into the forecourt, and Lord Seton emerged from the porch in leisurely fashion, cigarette in hand and spaniels at his heels. He raised a hand in greeting. Leaping out, Maurice Corden reciprocated with excessive bonhomie.

Brent, home of the Tirles since the fifteenth century, incorporated work of three architectural periods. The Elizabethan south wing included part of the original manor house. Projecting wings on the north side enclosed a courtyard, and had been completely rebuilt in the eighteenth century as a status symbol on the elevation of Sir William Tirle to the peerage. On coming into the title and estates, Roger Seton had put forward conversion plans which would enable four households to co-exist in complete independence. After much discussion and some heartburning the plans had been agreed upon by the immediate family circle. The Setons and the estate office now occupied the west wing, and Giles and Felicity Tirle the greater part of the eastern Georgian wing. Lady Arminel had a first-floor flat in the north-west angle, and Bill Emmett, the handyman and caretaker, was housed on the east side of the north gate into the courtyard, together with his wife, Elsie, and teenage daughter, Rosalie. The unoccupied state rooms were thus conveniently grouped in the rest of the Elizabethan and adjoining eastern Georgian wings, available for large-scale entertaining. They contained some valuable pictures, furniture and china, and an outstanding collection of miniatures. This included one of Charles the Second, commissioned by the monarch from Samuel Cooper, and presented by him to the lady of the house, together with a witty note alluding to favours received.

Lord Seton, keenly alive to the wind of economic change, had decided from the start to open Brent to the public, but also to keep the idea strictly to himself until the conversion of the house had been carried through. He was highly satisfied with the outcome of the latter. Not only was the general layout now practicable for escorted tours, but an invaluable supply of family power was assembled on the spot.

Maurice Corden, who missed little, congratulated him on his foresight, but the remark met with a cool reception.

'It was the only workable subdivision of the house if four families were to be fitted in. You've grasped the lie of the land remarkably quickly, Mr Corden.'

They were standing in the minstrels' gallery overlooking the great hall. Maurice Corden perched himself on the balustrade.

'I'll come clean,' he said chattily. 'Your write-up in *Country Life* three years ago. I always do my homework, you know. It impresses the not-quite-so-shrewd. Competent articles, weren't they, but a touch pedestrian?'

Lord Seton, who had personally approved the articles, made a non-committal reply, and remained standing. Maurice Corden shot a glance at him, but went on in a conversational vein.

'We'll do a lot better,' he said. 'Brent's going over big, you know. In my line of business you get to know if a place will tick. We've got the lot here, haven't we? Accessibility, picture-book setting, architectural interest and *such* props. . . . Everything to make the Great British Public feel it's getting its money's worth. We can risk a highish admission charge, I think. There are just one or two snags, of course. Circulation inside the house won't be too easy.'

'I foresaw that,' Lord Seton remarked. 'Nothing to be done about it, I'm afraid.'

'Not to worry,' Maurice Corden assured him. 'We had the same problem at Holchester, but Hermione Pomfret-Guille and I found a way out. Delightful people, she and John. I always drop in on them when I'm up that way. I daresay you'll run across them sometime. One of the oldest families in the north, you know.'

The violent banging of a door and hurried footsteps below made comment unnecessary. The next moment Giles Tirle appeared in the hall, hair ruffled and collar and tie askew.

'Mr Corden?' he called up urgently. 'Good show! I'm just back from Oxford. It's absolutely vital that we discuss the reconditioning of the old kitchen. My brother's jibbing at the expense, but in my view it's essential if we're going to show an authentic comprehensive picture of Tudor domestic life. I consider that we've a moral obligation to maintain authenticity . . .'

Lord Seton managed to get in a suggestion that the conversation could be conducted more easily on the ground floor.

In the screens passage, which linked forecourt and enclosed courtyard, Giles Tirle showed almost uncontrollable impatience to sweep Maurice Corden into the cavernous and derelict room opposite the hall.

'Just look at it!' he exclaimed. 'Think of the potential! There'll have to be preliminary treatment for damp, of course. It should never have been allowed to get into this state. It's a perfect example of its period. What, Roger? Supper? My wife hopes you'll join us, Mr Corden, and we'll be able to talk things over in peace. There's an enormous amount of work ahead. Half the stuff in the state rooms will have to be shifted round ...'

'Perfectly all right by us, Mr Corden.' There was barely concealed amusement in Lord Seton's eyes. 'Perhaps you'll have an opportunity of discussing the circulation problem with my sister-in-law. The idea is that she organises the escorted tours of the house.'

Bridget Seton glanced up enquiringly as her husband's image appeared in her dressing-table mirror.

'I've unloaded the fellow on to Felicity and Giles for supper,' he said, grinning broadly. 'We can eat on our own, thank God. If he survives, I'll take him off to the office again.'

'I do hope Felicity won't bait the unfortunate man. She was so naughty once or twice at lunch.' A faintly anxious expression came into Bridget's lovely face. 'You know, Roger, I'm sorry for him. It's being so desperately anxious to seem at ease that makes him say all the wrong things.'

'Save your pity for something more deserving, darling. He's impossible: the camaraderie, and the blatant name-dropping. But I admit he's first-class on the job. Sees possibilities in a flash, and knows about costs and returns. Anyway, I'll push him off after lunch to-morrow. Ready to come down? I badly need a drink.'

Over the coffee cups Felicity Tirle smiled winningly at her guest.

'You're the Writing on the Wall, Mr Corden, spelling out the horrors we've let ourselves in for with appalling clarity.'

'My dear lady, if you did but know how my heart bleeds for my distinguished clients. That after centuries of pride of place—'

'Not centuries where I'm concerned, Mr Corden. I'm

mere professional middle class. Jumped up, in fact.'

'The concept of class—' Giles began.

'Not now, darling,' Felicity said firmly. 'You haven't un-packed yet, and Mr Corden and I are going over the house to work out the best route for my escorted tours. Including the reconditioned Tudor kitchen, of course. Shall we go along now?'

Snatching up a notebook and pencil she led the way, abandoning her veiled banter. As they progressed through the state rooms it was borne in on her that Maurice Corden knew what he was talking about. He was surprisingly knowledgeable when it came to the contents of the rooms, too, and perceptive about items likely to have popular appeal. He's really quite tolerable in his own sphere, she thought. I wonder about the guide book ... If Giles does it on his own, either it won't be ready on time, or it'll read like a thesis for a Ph.D.

On the following morning Arminel Tirle, tracked down to one of the greenhouses, confronted her brother across boxes of seedlings.

'Do I have to come and discuss things with this man Corden?' she demanded.

'For heaven's sake, Arminel,' replied Lord Seton. 'Ob-viously you must be in on decisions about access and outside amenities, as Corden calls them. Unless you want to contract out, that is.'

'You know perfectly well I don't want to contract out.'

'All right. Well come on, then. He's waiting for us in the park.'

She followed unwillingly, and they cut through the market garden towards the north-east angle of the house in silence.

'Why this side? What does he want to do?'

'Open up the east gate and drive, instead of bringing people in up the main drive. I hadn't thought of it myself, but it's got points.'

Rounding the corner they came into a formal garden

enclosed from the park by a box hedge. Beyond it Maurice Corden was inspecting the disused drive in a canary-yellow pullover and light, tight trousers. Catching sight of them he waved enthusiastically and came striding up to the gate, a large folder under his arm.

'Good morning, Lady Arminel! How delightful to meet again! Of course the O.C. Grounds must be in on these weighty decisions.'

A slim erect figure in earthy dungarees, Lady Arminel eyed him coolly down the distinctive Tirle nose.

'Good morning, Mr Corden. Actually my status is manager of my brother's market garden. On a commission basis.'

'It's this important access question we've got to consider,' Lord Seton interposed urbanely. 'How do you feel now that you've had a look at the surface of the old drive?'

'Still definitely in favour of the entry on this side. Admittedly it will cost something to open up, but much less in the long term than letting coaches rip up the long front drive.'

Lady Arminel gave an almost involuntary nod of approval, which was not lost on Maurice Corden. He opened his folder and placed it carefully on the top of the box hedge.

'There's a more subtle aspect of salesmanship involved, too,' he continued. 'We need to preserve the mystique of the Stately, you know. People who come to see a place like this simply wallow in it. Such a mistake to let them come lurching up the front drive wedged in their coaches, half-suffocated by diesel fumes and lack of fresh air, and getting used to that dramatic—that utterly gorgeous Elizabethan façade as they approach. Bad psychology. Let them in on this side, be just a trifle daunted at first by Palladian austerity, and then walk round to the forecourt to find that their image of a real live Stately was right after all. It's always an Elizabethan image in the popular mind, you know.'

There was a silence in which his hearers mentally registered agreement with his thesis and dislike of its flamboyant presentation.

'That side road's narrow,' Lord Seton remarked, with apparent inconsequence. 'Carries quite a bit of traffic across the downs, too. I don't know what the police reaction would be.'

Maurice Corden raised a tentative eyebrow.

'Dare I even suggest one or two passing places notched out of the ancestral acres?'

Ignoring him, Lord Seton turned to his sister.

'What's your reaction? We should have to go into the question of retention of legal rights, of course.'

'Provided the ground could be recovered at any future date it seems a practical solution.'

'Retention of legal rights,' murmured Maurice Corden, his face bent over his folder as he made a note. He straightened up again and surveyed the park. 'The car park here, then? I suggest the ticket office about here, and the route round to the forecourt marked by movable guard rails. Outside the hedge, of course, to spare Mr and Mrs Giles....'

Presently they moved round to the north side of the house, to consider the conversion of an adjacent barn into a tea room. To Lord Seton's relief his sister raised no difficulties. He decided that it was inexpedient to raise the question of the shop which he hoped to persuade her to run for visitors. She was decidedly high horse this morning.

Quite suddenly Lady Arminel cut into a discussion of the siting of the essential lavatory block.

'I want the shop immediately opposite the north gate,' she said. 'It will catch people's eye as they come through.'

Momentarily caught off balance at achieving his aim so effortlessly, Lord Seton quickly recovered himself.

'Shop?' he queried diplomatically.

'Of course we shall have to have a shop. All the successful places do. I've written round. Properly run, and selling garden produce as well as the usual run of things, it pays.'

Maurice Corden looked at her with unwilling admiration.

'My dear lady, you've beaten me at the post. The Brent Shop was to be my final suggestion. You must let me design you a little boutique. Nothing olde worlde or twee, of course. Just simple and functional, don't you think?'

'Thank you, Mr Corden, but I've already got out my own design.'

'Well,' said Lord Seton, 'if we're all in agreement about the siting of these various buildings, I think we can call it a day. You'll let me have your detailed report as soon as you can get it out, I take it? We mustn't be late for lunch. You must be anxious to get off.'

Once set in motion, preparations for the opening of the house gathered momentum at a surprising rate. During the next twelve months the family became increasingly involved in their various assignments. Maurice Corden paid a second visit to discuss advance publicity, and a third, as Felicity had foreseen would be necessary, when Giles became completely bogged down over the guide book. There were a series of crises of different kinds, all of which were eventually weathered, and the venture was triumphantly launched on Easter Monday.

It was a success from the start.

'How come the show biz has caught on so well without gimmicks?' Robert Tirle asked his mother, as he contemplated the crowd of visitors one afternoon in his summer vacation.

'Geography partly,' she answered. 'We're in a holiday area, and easy to get to. And there's a lot for the culture-seekers, too. They come and revel, and go away quite starry-eyed. And don't forget all the preliminary work we've put in, my lad.'

Robert, a shrewdly amused eighteen, laughed.

'Uncle Roger's sanitary block?'

'Certainly. A dear old soul told me the other day that

our loos were the best she'd ever come across on an outing. You needn't be so superior. Your father nearly killed himself getting the state rooms sorted out, and restoring the Tudor kitchen. All for your benefit in the long run, may I point out?'

CHAPTER TWO

BY THE third summer the routine of an open day was functioning automatically. On a certain Tuesday in the first half of July it began to tick over as usual with the arrival of the cleaning women from the village of Brenting close by. They walked up to the house in a group, volubly discussing medical topics. In the staff cloakroom they donned overalls, and then vanished to their assignments.

Lady Arminel had already been at work for some time. Having interviewed the head gardener at eight sharp, she was now rapidly snipping off dead blooms in the rose garden.

'Mornin', m'lady.'

She glanced up to see old Sam Webber. He was engaged on his morning round of clearing the litter baskets, and brandished an empty beer bottle for her inspection.

'Found 'e plonked down slap in the middle o' the maze, I did,' he told her.

'Somebody must have been celebrating having got there,' she suggested. 'Had many calls for help lately, Sam?'

He gave a fat chuckle.

'Proper confloption some of 'em gets into, thinkin' the coach'll go without 'em.'

'You wicked old man,' she said appreciatively.

He chuckled again, touched his forelock, and went off happily.

In the office the telephone rang shrilly. Peggy Blackmore, Lord Seton's secretary picked up the receiver.

'Blennerhasset's, Mrs Blackmore,' said a familiar masculine voice. 'Joe Hill here. The usual's booked right up for this afternoon, and we'd like to send you a later trip, arriving 4.45. All right?'

'Will they have had tea, Joe?'

'Sure. Panoramic coastal drive and tea at the Wreckers, ending up with you.'

'That's fine, then. We'll lay on guides. Thanks for letting us know.'

'Pleasure, Mrs Blackmore. Any time. Goodbye for now, then.'

Peggy Blackmore dialled the tea room on the house telephone. As she waited she watched a gardener pushing a handcart heaped with delphiniums across the courtyard. Everything going smoothly, she thought contentedly.

'Blennerhasset's are sending a full coach this afternoon, Mrs Treddle,' she said, in response to a quack in her ear. 'And a later one after tea, at about a quarter to five. They'll want icecreams, I expect. Sorry it's a bit near closing time.'

'Thanks a lot, Mrs Blackmore,' came the sharpish voice of the manageress. 'No trouble at all, as long as people do their work properly. That Rosalie Emmett's not here yet, if you please, and she's only got to step outside the gate. Young people just couldn't care less these days, and what the world's going to—'

Peggy Blackmore was briefly soothing, and disengaged herself, her unoccupied ear having detected Lord Seton's arrival in his private office beyond the communicating door. Her heart beat a shade faster. A few moments later he came in wearing city clothes, and smoking an after-breakfast cigarette.

'How are the tickets going for "Brent by Candlelight"?' he asked, after some casual conversation.

'Like hot cakes,' she replied. 'It's going over in a big way. Mulled wine in the Tudor kitchen was an absolute inspiration of yours, Lord Seton. I suppose it's too late to fix a repeat later in the season?'

'I wonder,' he said thoughtfully. 'Let's have a look at the fixture list.'

Gathering up the morning's mail, she followed him into his office, and they became immersed in their usual routine.

After carrying out her daily inspection of the public rooms Lady Seton devoted herself to flower arrangement, for which she had talent. Working with confidence she happily built up a spectacular display of delphiniums in the huge fireplace of the hall. At intervals she remembered that she was on call for guide duty on Tuesdays, and devoutly hoped that she would not be needed.

In the course of the morning tradesmen's vans arrived, disgorged supplies and departed again. The fragrant smell of home-baked scones came from the kitchen at the rear of the tea room. The rattle of Peggy Blackmore's typewriter floated out of the office window, punctuating the croodling of fantail pigeons. Soon after eleven Lord Seton emerged, and drove off at speed to catch the London train at Crockmouth for a board meeting of one of his companies. Lady Arminel opened up the shop. She replenished the postcard stands and stacks of guide books, and set out a tempting display of soft fruit, plants and honey.

Activity further increased from one o'clock onwards. Sam Webber returned from his dinner metamorphosed into a car park attendant. The ticket office, which controlled the entry of visitors, was manned by a Mrs Moore from the village. Felicity Tirle, who organised the work of the guides, came down to their room at the north gate, and discussed the afternoon's bookings with Molly Danvers and Jane Willis, two retired schoolmistresses who were on duty with her.

As the courtyard clock struck two, Sam Webber ceremoniously opened the gate of the car park and admitted a coach from Huddersfield, four private cars, the occupants of which eyed the coach party with unconcealed dismay, and two earnest hikers armed with maps and guide books.

These early arrivals were followed by a steady stream of later ones all through the afternoon. Voices, bursts of laughter, footsteps in the forecourt and the distant sound of cars coming and going formed a background against which Lady Seton sat writing letters in the seclusion of the private wing. From time to time she glanced out of the window, her hopes rising as the afternoon wore on and no summons came.

At four o'clock her daughters' former nanny brought in her tea on a trolley. She was an active little woman with bright eyes, known to the family as Ping.

'If it's crowded like this already, m'lady, whatever will it be like in August?' she demanded, looking down on the forecourt.

'More crowded still, I hope, Ping,' said Bridget Seton loyally, getting up from her bureau. 'We're doing very well, you know. His lordship's pleased. I wish August wasn't the children's holidays, though. It's rather hard on them.'

Ping, a devotee of Bridget's, remarked drily that it was hard on other people, too, and she hoped her ladyship wasn't going to be called on in all this heat.

Left alone, Bridget relaxed over her tea, letting her eyes wander happily round her beautiful drawing room. Her love for Brent was combined with an intuitive appreciation which she was incapable of expressing, and which would have astonished the rest of the family, who teased her about her inability to remember dates and distinguish schools of painting and architectural periods.

If only I'd had a son, she thought, part of me would have gone on here as long as Setons keep the house . . . If only I'd heard them say 'you've got such a lovely little *boy*, Lady Seton,' when I came out of the anaesthetic. . . .

She started as the house telephone rang.

'Awfully sorry, Biddy,' came Felicity's voice, 'but we're going to be swamped for the last hour. A wretched man has just rung up who wants to bring a scout camp over at half-past four, and a late Blennerhasset's coming at a quarter to five. I think Molly Danvers and I had better take on the scouts, if you and Jane could split the coach party, and tack on any oddments who turn up. Can you bear it?'

'Of course I can,' Bridget assured her, stifling her disappointment and apprehension. 'Tell Jane I'll be in the forecourt at twenty to five.'

'Splendid. They'll only be Blennerhasset run-of-the-mill, I'm sure. Don't bother about dates and so on. Just concentrate on human interest: they'll lap it up.'

As Lady Seton arrived, a party emerged from the house in the wake of Jane Willis. The latter, experienced in handling humanity in the mass, quickly disengaged herself and came forward, a welcoming smile on her agreeable, if unremarkable face.

'Good afternoon, Lady Seton,' she said. 'I'm so sorry you've had to be brought in. It's been simply non-stop, but this lot will be the last, anyway. We shall have the usual job over splitting them up, I expect. They'll all want to go round with you, of course.'

'With me?' echoed Bridget Seton, in genuine astonishment.

'Why, yes.' Jane Willis looked at her, momentarily at a loss. 'It's your home, you see,' she added rather lamely, feeling that it would be familiar to comment on the beauty and elegance which she admired so much. 'Heavens, here they come already.'

They walked forward to greet the vanguard of the party as it came round the east side of the house.

In a surprisingly short space of time Jane had jollied everyone into two groups of roughly equal size. As she moved off with one, she casually informed the members of the other that they were being taken round by Lady Seton herself. Bridget, with a feeling of being abandoned to her fate, became aware of a sea of curious faces. They appeared to belong mainly to well-upholstered elderly women with permanently waved and blued hair. There was a minority of men in holiday garb, hung around with cameras and other photographic equipment. Far too diffident to interpret their stares as a compliment, she braced herself for the ordeal.

'I'm delighted to welcome you all to Brent,' she told them untruthfully, but with a charming smile. 'Perhaps you would like to begin by looking at the outside of the house?'

No one spoke, but all faced about with a good deal of shuffling.

'This is the oldest part of the house,' she told them. 'It was mostly built in the reign of the first Queen Elizabeth, when it was the fashion to build your house in the shape of an E. But if you look carefully you'll see that the middle part of the E is different from the rest. It's much older. The stone is a different colour, and the windows are not the same.'

Her audience made gratified murmurs at being able to detect the difference, and cameras clicked.

'Would this middle section go back to Henry the Eighth's time?' enquired a thin man with a prominent Adam's apple.

Bridget Seton seized thankfully on this universally recognised landmark in English history.

'Even before his time,' she replied confidently. 'The old house which the Elizabethan builders included in the new one was quite a simple affair. If we go inside now, I can show you what it was like.'

By this time Jane Willis's party had moved on into the hall, which housed the family portraits, and Bridget led hers into the huge fifteenth-century kitchen to the left of the screens passage, which had been rescued from its damp and derelict condition by Giles, replastered and whitewashed, and provided with as much period equipment as he had been able to collect. To her relief there were no searching questions about the purpose of some of the odderlooking items, and her carefully memorised description of a Tudor banquet went down well. A look through the door showed her that the party ahead had moved on again, and she rallied her own and conducted it into the hall.

Unlike Felicity, who was both informative and diverting

about the portraits, Bridget invariably found herself tongue-tied at this point. Her sense of kinship with Brent's past inhabitants made it intolerable to her to discuss them with a crowd of unconcerned strangers. It was here that the nightmare feeling of a party disintegrating and getting out of control always descended upon her, and today was no exception. People lingered obstinately to admire the delphiniums, and she suddenly caught sight of the thin man with the Adam's apple in the act of stepping over the red cord which barred the newel staircase leading up to the gallery.

'I'm afraid that staircase isn't open to the public,' she called to him. 'The treads are too worn and slippery.'

The offender desisted rather ungraciously under the stares of the rest of the party, and a distinct constraint developed.

'Shall we start on the portraits now?' she suggested desperately. 'This is Sir Matthew Tirle, who lived in the reign of Elizabeth the First.' She indicated a burly beruffed figure with a piratical air. 'He was a great friend of Sir Walter Raleigh, who first brought tobacco to England, didn't he, and—er—potatoes?'

The faces turned to her ranged from the politely un-moved to the frankly bored. In despair she hurried over the portraits, and tried to arouse interest by describing the part played by the hall in the life of a fifteenth-century household. Apart from a few clicks of the tongue from some of the women, even this fell flat. Finally she led the way towards the library, leaving too small a gap between Jane Willis's party and her own. As a result the two groups began to reunite, and became hopelessly mixed up. A traffic block developed on the stairs, where Felicity Tirle and perspiring scouts were trying to make their way down against the tide. Bridget, always very conscious of her sister-in-law's competence, felt miserably humiliated by the confusion for which she was largely responsible. She tried to catch Felicity's eye apologetically, but failed.

At the top of the staircase Jane Willis took the situation firmly in hand.

'Now, it's a case of follow-your-leader if we're all going to see the rest of the house comfortably,' she proclaimed. 'My lot this way to see the miniatures and the priest's hiding hole first, please, while Lady Seton's go with her to the old chapel and the Tudor bedrooms. Then we'll change over.'

To Bridget's astonishment there was instant compliance, and her party showed an unexpected interest in the tiny chapel and the Elizabethan beds and hangings. Only one more river to cross, she thought thankfully, as they arrived in the miniatures room at last. Here, too, everything went well. The hidden catch releasing the sliding panel over the entrance to the priest's hole worked easily, and Charles the Second's gift to Henrietta Tirle exercised its usual fascination. After several unobtrusive glances at her watch the moment came at which she felt justified in making a start for the ground floor.

'The house will be closing in ten minutes,' she announced, trying to be audible above the babble, 'but the grounds are open until six o'clock if you care to walk round the gardens and try the maze.'

'Oh my! Suppose we can't get out again?' enquired an anxious voice.

There was general laughter in which Bridget joined, and she was reassuring as she led the chattering crowd down the staircase and out into the courtyard. Here she indicated the way to the shop and the tea room, answered a few questions including a timid one about toilets, and after receiving some rather incoherent thanks stood watching a rapid dispersal through the north gate. With a sigh of relief she turned back into the house, and stood listening in the screens passage. After the tramping of feet and buzz of conversation the silence was balm. In a moment the half-hour would chime, and there would be the reassuring sound of Emmett shutting the gate, the first stage in the nightly return of peace and security.

The chimes rang out, faintly melancholy, and were followed in a matter of seconds by two heavy thuds as the big double gates were pushed home and bolted. Immediately after came the purposeful step of Bill Emmett crossing the courtyard on his way to secure the front door and the public rooms.

'Evening, m'lady,' he said, catching sight of Bridget. 'Proper crowd it's bin this afternoon. More like August than July, wouldn't you say?'

Bridget agreed.

'By the way,' she told him, 'we may be rather late getting back tonight. We're dining over at Fulminster.'

'Very good, m'lady. I'll take a turn with the dog last thing, just to have a look round.'

CHAPTER THREE

SOMETIMES privileged persons were taken over Brent when the house was officially closed. They were usually invited by Giles Tirle, and were specialists in some field of architecture or art, but now and again a friend would ask leave to bring an interested guest. A fixture of this kind had been made for the following morning. A near neighbour, Sir James Mallaby, and an American senator and his wife who were staying with him were lunching with the Setons after a tour of the house.

The guests arrived just before eleven. Kurt Lessinger was tall, gaunt and clinically clean-looking, and his wife Saidie, a typically smart and purposeful American woman, both in their fifties. After the introductions Sir James begged himself off the tour.

'I've simply got to get advice from Arminel,' he explained. 'An extraordinary blight has started up on some of my apple trees. No, don't bother, Roger. I'll soon run her to earth.'

'It's vurry, vurry good of you to let us take up your valuable time, Lord Seton,' Kurt Lessinger said as his host departed. 'My wife and I count it a vurry great privilege to visit you and Lady Seton in your histahric home.'

He beamed as his admiring gaze comprehended Bridget and the Elizabethan façade.

'We're both delighted to have this opportunity of meeting you,' she told him. 'My husband's going to take you round: he knows far more about Brent than I do, and then we'll all meet again for drinks before lunch. Don't lose all count of time, will you, Roger?'

It soon became clear to Lord Seton that the Lessingers were not merely enthusiastic, but unusually well-informed. An hour slipped away agreeably, almost unnoticed. Suddenly surfacing, he realised that he must speed things up.

'I particularly want you to see the miniatures,' he said, tactfully prising them out of a bedroom with interesting tapestries. 'It's quite a good collection. It used to be in the library, which was a better setting, but we moved it up here when we opened the house, for greater security.'

'Don't you live in dread of burglaries with all these marvellous heirlooms around, Lord Seton?' asked Mrs Lessinger.

'Security's a bit of a headache, certainly,' he admitted. 'Country house robberies are getting much too popular with the criminal classes. But you can't hope to make a place like this completely burglar-proof. We just take all possible precautions, and hope for the best.'

'Do you have a night watchman?' Kurt Lessinger enquired.

'No, we don't, actually. We've got some valuable stuff here, but not on the scale of the great houses, of course. And a factor which weighs with our insurance company is that quite a few people live in various parts of the house—there are four different households, in fact.'

'All the same, I guess I'd be hearing noises all the night through,' Mrs Lessinger said, as she went through a door held open for her by Lord Seton. 'Is this where you have the love token King Charles Second gave your lady ancestor?'

'It is. Over here, in this showcase, with a compromising note from His Majesty. History doesn't relate her husband's reactions—if he knew anything about it, that is.'

Fascinated, the Lessingers pored over this and other exhibits.

'Wal, Lord Seton,' Kurt said, straightening up, 'I'll say that guide book of yours is just one long British understatement. Why, if we had a house like yours back in the

States . . . And didn't I read about a priest's hiding hole dating back to the first Queen Elizabeth?'

'You did. It's built within the fifteenth-century outer wall, which is very thick. The entrance is behind a sliding panel, released by a spring hidden in the carving.'

He led the way across the room, explaining that a steep flight of steps led down to a little chamber measuring about five feet by four.

'If you could just go down on one knee here, Mrs Lessinger,' he said, 'I'll press, and you'll find you can shift the panel to the left, across the window recess, and look right down. We've fixed a light to come on automatically.'

'Now, if this isn't just too cute,' she exclaimed, taking up her position.

There was a faint click, and the panel moved easily. Saidie Lessinger leant forward with keen interest. She remained immobile without speaking, and then stood up abruptly, a startled expression on her face.

'I'll say it's lifelike,' she said a little shakily, 'But why do you have the figure in modern dress?'

The two men stared at her.

'Just one moment . . .'

Lord Seton took a swift step forward and dropped on to his knees. Withdrawing his head again, his eyes encountered Kurt Lessinger's.

'I'm afraid there's been an accident,' he said.

Lord Seton's opinion of his guests rose further as he hastily escorted them to the private wing. Although badly shocked Mrs Lessinger was controlled, and her husband only anxious to be of some use.

'Can the poor guy possibly be alive?' he asked.

'I think it's out of the question,' Lord Seton replied. 'You see, he must have been lying there since the house closed at half-past five yesterday afternoon . . . I can only say how appalled I am that Mrs Lessinger and yourself have run into this situation . . . No, I insist on your staying to lunch with my wife, even if I'm tied up with the police, who'll have to be notified at once.'

Against worrying background thoughts of legal liability and insurance cover, and the prospect of having to close for the afternoon, he handed the Lessingers over to his wife with a brief explanation. Her horrified expression startled him, but she quickly recovered herself and concentrated on the visitors. Leaving them with her he hurried back to the miniatures room. Another look into the priest's hole convinced him that the man was dead, but he decided that he must make sure before taking further steps. He took off his coat, backed into the narrow opening, and descended as if on a ladder. At the bottom it was difficult to find a foothold without actually standing on the huddled body, but he managed to turn round, and leant forward to investigate.

A few moments later he re-emerged, his face set. Mechanically dusting down his trousers and putting on his coat, he stood staring unseeingly at his dirty hands, his mind moving rapidly. Then he turned quickly and went out of the room, locking the door and pocketing the key. Downstairs in his office he made the first 999 call of his life, and asked for Police.

'Crockmouth Police Headquarters,' came a voice in a matter of seconds.

'Lord Seton, speaking from Brent,' he said calmly. 'We've just found a man in our priest's hole. He's dead, and it looks as though his neck's broken.'

'We'll be over right away, my lord,' replied the voice, a trace of excitement discernible in the stock response.

Replacing the receiver, Lord Seton took up the house telephone.

'Roger here,' he said when Felicity Tirle answered. 'Come down to the office, will you? It's urgent.'

He heard a sharp intake of breath before she answered that she would come at once and immediately rang off.

As he returned from hastily washing his hands they met in the passage. In response to the anxious enquiry in her

34

face he indicated the communicating door into the secretary's office.

'Peggy's got to be in on it, too,' he said, striding across the room.

As they came in Peggy Blackmore got up quickly, looking surprised.

'Something extremely serious has happened,' he told them both bluntly. 'A dead man has been found down the priest's hole. I think he's broken his neck.'

The two women stared at him, speechless.

'I've rung the police,' he went on, 'and they'll be here in about ten minutes. Obviously we shall have to close this afternoon, and the immediate problem is the best way to set about it. What parties have booked?'

Peggy Blackmore gave a quick glance at Felicity, who seemed bereft of speech, and consulted a diary on her desk.

'Three coaches from a distance,' she said. 'They'd be difficult to contact as late as this. And one Blennerhasset.'

'I suggest we leave well alone until the police come,' Felicity said, abruptly coming to life. 'We could ask them to put a man at the visitors' entrance to answer questions and cope with the Press. We shall have newsmen swarming all over the place if we aren't careful. They'll soon start ringing up, anyway.'

'If the telephones were all switched through to me,' put in Peggy Blackmore, 'I could give a stock answer to everybody.'

'I doubt if the Press can be fobbed off as easily as that,' said Lord Seton grimly. 'Still, it's a sound idea. I'll ask the police to draft a bare statement, and you could say it was official. With any luck they'll send Inspector Diplock. He's a decent co-operative sort of chap. I absolutely agree that the more we all keep out of it the better.'

Felicity looked relieved.

'But what about our own people this afternoon? Tea room staff, and guides and Emmett, for instance?'

'Better not to say anything until we know how much disruption we're in for. If we can tell them everything will be back to normal tomorrow they won't get so rattled. Good God, I'd forgotten Arminel for the moment. Will you find her, and tell her what's happened? And by the way, who took the last party round yesterday? I could see a camera by the body, so it seems fairly obvious that the man came in as a visitor, and managed to slope off.'

'Lady Seton and Jane Willis,' Felicity said unwillingly.

Dr Ross, the police surgeon, was a big man with formidably bushy eyebrows. He extricated himself from the opening in the panelling with difficulty, dusty and red in the face. His expression suggested that but for Lord Seton's presence he would have commented uninhibitedly.

'The man's dead all right,' he said tersely. 'Broken neck, but I'm not committing myself about the cause of death until I've had a proper look at him. It's impossible down there.'

'Can you give an approximate idea of the time of death?' asked Inspector Diplock.

Dr Ross scowled at him.

'Hardly a reasonable question under the circumstances, I should have thought. Rigor's just beginning to go off, but how can I tell what the conditions are like in that place? Certainly not less than six hours ago, and Lord Seton's told us that the body couldn't have been there before the last lot of visitors had a look, at about five-fifteen yesterday afternoon. See here, you're going to have quite a job getting him up. I suggest I go home to my lunch and my afternoon surgery, and come back in a couple of hours. There's no point in my hanging around here.'

'All right,' agreed the Inspector. 'Only don't make it longer than a couple of hours. We'll have taken some photographs and got him up for you by then.'

With a brief bow to Lord Seton, Dr Ross made for the

door, which was opened for him by a constable standing unobtrusively in the background.

'I'd be glad of the use of a telephone, my lord,' Inspector Diplock said, glancing thoughtfully round the room. 'We shall have to bring in reinforcements. Perhaps while I'm contacting the Super, you would make arrangements for closing to the public this afternoon? I'm sorry, but you'll understand that it's unavoidable, the way things are.'

Roger Seton led the way, suppressing his annoyance at the feeling of being under authority in his own house.

Inspector Diplock's reinforcements were considerable. By mid-afternoon the forecourt of Brent contained a whole assortment of official vehicles, including a mortuary van. At intervals Lord Seton flung down *The Times* and went over to the drawing room window to survey the scene.

'What the hell are they doing all this time?' he demanded at last.

Felicity Tirle, sprawled in an armchair, lit another cigarette and drew on it deeply.

'Getting the body up must be tricky,' she remarked. 'And I should think they took a lot of photographs for the coroner first, with somebody hanging on to the photographer's heels.'

Lady Seton, a taut figure with head bent over her embroidery, gave a small shudder of distaste. Since the departure of Sir James Mallaby and the Lessingers after brief interviews with Inspector Diplock, she had said little, beyond insisting that her incompetence as a guide was entirely responsible for the disaster. Attempts by the others to challenge this conclusion had availed nothing. Returning to his chair, her husband sat looking at her unhappily for a few moments, before recovering *The Times* from the floor and crackling its pages impatiently.

An unmistakable sense of the police having taken over dominated the house. The main gate had been locked, and a stolid constable stood at the visitors' entrance, confronting a growing crowd of disappointed tourists and curious villagers. In the house itself, the tension of its normal inhabitants expressed itself in various ways. Peggy Blackmore made valiant efforts to get on with her work, distracted by nervous dread of the next telephone call. Incredibly, the news of the dramatic discovery of the body had already reached the London offices of the national newspapers, and she was finding it increasingly difficult to parry the fire of leading questions. She suddenly broke into a sweat at the thought of the next morning's headlines, and ripped a letter containing several mistakes from her typewriter. As she did so, the telephone rang...

Bill Emmett, looking worried, kept making pointless sorties from the caretaker's quarters. His normal routine suspended, he seemed completely at a loss.

'Settle to something, for pity's sake,' said his wife, who was doing some mending. 'What's happened's no fault of yours. 'Tisn't as though you're an X-ray, to see what's going on through stone walls.'

' 'Tisn't that, as you know very well,' he retorted. 'It's what's bound to come out, once the police get to askin' questions. How much longer's Rosalie goin' to be over to the tea room kitchen?'

'Till all the jam's made. Lady A's not having the day's soft fruit for the shop wasted, just because there's no visitors. Never wastes nothing—not her time, neither. She's stocktaking. The others is sitting round in the drawing room, Mrs Pringle says.'

Muttering something about his workshop, Bill Emmett went out once more. As he came through the gate he distracted Lady Arminel, who lost count of her reserve of souvenir tea towels as she watched him.

At four o'clock precisely a macabre resurrection took place in the miniatures room. Sergeant Green and Constable Forbes mopped their brows triumphantly, and Inspector Diplock heaved a sigh of relief.

'You nip down and bring up the camera, and anything else that's down there, Forbes,' he ordered. 'Now then, doctor, we'll get him on to the stretcher for you.'

Dr Ross, disgruntled by the ban on smoking, advanced on the body without enthusiasm. Everything, the Inspector reflected with some satisfaction, had really gone according to plan. As soon as the doctor had made his preliminary examination they'd see if the chap's name was on him, and then the body would go off to the mortuary, and Lord Seton would be told that he could open as usual tomorrow.

There was a purposeful step in the passage, and Inspector Diplock swung round indignantly, to find himself confronting Major Egerton, the Chief Constable.

'Afternoon, Diplock. Afternoon, Ross,' announced the new arrival, with a nod to other ranks present. 'I chanced to drop in at Crockmouth, and heard about this rum business. Bit of a job getting him up, eh?'

Inspector Diplock, torn between disappointment at not being left to cope on his own, and relief at the appearance of a superior, began to enumerate the steps he had taken.

'Before we moved him, sir, we—'

He was interrupted by a muffled booming which seemed to come from the bowels of the earth.

'Good grief, what's that?' demanded Major Egerton.

'Constable Forbes, sir,' replied the Inspector, chagrined by the ludicrous effect produced by one of his men. 'I sent him down to bring up a camera.'

He strode across the room.

'Can't hear a word you're saying, Forbes,' he called down with asperity. 'Come up and make a proper report if it's necessary ... What? ... Well, pass up one thing at a time then, can't you?'

Turning to the Chief Constable he explained that Forbes had found a lot of other stuff as well as the camera. The next moment a dusty but still inflated air cushion was thrust through the opening in the panelling, followed by a camera, a powerful electric torch, an almost empty whisky flask, some sandwiches, an illustrated guide to Brent and a small rucksack. Inspector Diplock whipped open the latter, and extracted a nylon rope ladder, strips of mica of various sizes, a screwdriver, and sundry other tools found useful by the housebreaking fraternity.

'So what?' demanded Major Egerton. 'It's exactly the same technique as that coins robbery at Wonbridge Castle in the spring. The chap came in as a tourist, hid up somewhere in the house, and came out and did his stuff when they'd closed down for the night.'

Inspector Diplock whistled.

'Looks like the same chap, all right. I wonder what happened? Could he have had a coronary, shinning up those steps?'

'He could have, but he didn't.'

They turned round quickly. Keen professional interest had replaced Dr Ross's disgruntled boredom.

'I clambered down into that bloody deathtrap myself this morning. It was obvious that the man had gone clean over backwards, fracturing his skull and breaking his neck when he landed at the bottom. So I can't see how he got this hefty bruise on his chest. Take a look.'

The four policemen crowded round.

'Are you saying someone landed him a hefty wallop in the chest which sent him over?' Major Egerton stared at the doctor.

'Off the record, it looks rather like it. Officially I'm saying that the bruise is compatible with a violent blow in the chest. The experts will tell you if it was made by a fist or a weapon of some sort. I'd say the latter.'

There was a startled silence, broken only by the heavy breathing of Sergeant Green, who had edged nearer to get a better view.

'Well, this clinches it.' The Chief Constable was suddenly decisive. 'Here's an assault with fatal results—perhaps by an accomplice—on a chap who'd come here to commit a robbery. And the robbery technique's the same as that used in other country house break-ins lately. I'm sorry if you're going to be disappointed, Diplock, but this is a job which needs the Yard's facilities. As soon as I've contacted the Super, I'm going to ring them.'

'OK by me, sir,' replied Inspector Diplock in a tone of relief.

CHAPTER FOUR

'Of course, the pathologist's report may knock the bottom out of the case,' the Assistant Commissioner remarked to Detective-Superintendent Tom Pollard. 'At the moment we've only the police surgeon's opinion that the bruise on the chest couldn't have been made by the fall. But all the same, the chap was all lined up to bring off a carefully planned robbery, and if the passport they found on him is really his, he's normally resident abroad. It was issued by our consulate in Buenos Aires. An overseas link might come in useful if it transpires that the business was meant to be another of these country house thefts. I think you'd better go down and see what you make of it, Pollard. You'll be on the spot if the pathologist decides somebody landed this Raymond Peplow a hefty wallop, and if he doesn't, you can look into the robbery aspect. You haven't anything important on hand, as you've only just got back —having had a rattling good holiday, from the look of you. Where did you go?'

'Down to our old haunts, sir: a farmhouse in the Wiltshire Downs. We had super weather, and a real let-up. The emotional appeal of twins paid dividends—the farmer's wife would have taken them over altogether, if we'd let her.'

'Nature's compensation to their parents, I imagine. Well, you'd better get off to this Stately Home with the usual support, as soon as you've set the obvious enquiries in train. Good luck.'

Pollard withdrew decorously, but once outside the room his brow furrowed, and he strode along the corridors to his own office with an energy indicating exasperation. Others, he reflected, got scooped up out of their home life at the drop of a hat. Doctors, for instance, emergency service workers. Politicians if a crisis blew up. But if whatever it was went on for any length of time they'd be relieved, whereas he'd be saddled with this affair until it was either cleared up or shelved ... Only yesterday morning they'd been having a normal family life down on the farm.

'I'm off to Midshire,' he told his secretary briefly. 'A place called Brent. Get Sergeant Toye, will you, and rustle up anything I ought to do before we start?'

Toye, pale and impassive, materialised like magic, was briefed, and disappeared again to alert Detective-Constables Boyce and Strickland, the technicians of the team, and see about a car. Pollard grabbed a pad, and drafted requests for information about Raymond Peplow to be sent to Interpol and the British Consul in Buenos Aires. He then read through and signed the papers put in front of him, and sat in thought for a few moments.

'Get me a copy of *Who's Who,* will you, Blake?'

As the secretary vanished Pollard dialled his home in Wimbledon. The Italian au pair answered.

'*Il Soprintendente!*' she exclaimed enthusiastically. 'I fetch Signora Poll-llarrd for you.'

He heard clicketty heels and flying footsteps, and then his wife Jane running lightly down the stairs.

'Not already?' she asked, dismay in her voice.

'Afraid so, darling. We're just off to Midshire. Shall I quit? I feel like it at the moment.'

'It helps one along to know there's always the option, doesn't it? Any idea if it's likely to be a long job?'

'Not a clue. It's begun like an improbable stage thriller, but could tie up with other things. There may be a para in the evening paper. A Stately Home called Brent.'

'Well, that sounds a bit less repulsive than a back street in a slum, anyway. The local colour could be quite intriguing. Take care, though, won't you?'

'Take care yourself, Mrs Pollard, mother of twins. All well?'

'Very well. We're just bedding them down. One thing, there isn't much time for repining when you're away.'

'I'll ring sometime tomorrow. I ought to have some idea of what I'm in for by then. Blast and damn everything! Here's Blake coming back. Bless you.'

Pollard flicked hastily through the pages of *Who's Who*.

'SETON, 8th Earl of, c.1762,' he read. 'Roger Delamotte Tirle...Coldstream Guards...b. Oct. 1st 1919...eldest surv. s. of 7th Earl...two ds...served 1939-45 war...Deputy Chairman Colett-Winthorpe Construction Co...Director Forrest Foods, Houseware Amalgamated ...Clubs ...Recreations ... Heir: bro. Hon. Giles Tirle...Residence, Brent, Midshire.'

He shut the book as the expected summons came from the box on his desk, picked up his overnight case and murder bag, and made for the door.

Familiar with slightly resentful and even suspicious receptions from local forces, Pollard was agreeably surprised by the businesslike atmosphere at Crockmouth police headquarters. He learnt that the area pathologist had nearly finished the post-mortem, and would look in to make a brief verbal report before leaving. Inspector Diplock was introduced by Major Egerton as the chap who had been in on the affair from the start.

'I hope he's going to stay in on it, for the moment at any rate,' Pollard said, liking the Inspector's air of solidity and commonsense. 'The Yard may have wide facilities, but we depend entirely on you local people for the set-up.'

Inspector Diplock looked surprised and gratified, and replied that he would be glad to be of any assistance he could.

Dr Netley, the pathologist, appeared as Pollard and Toye were tackling the beer and sandwiches thoughtfully provided by Superintendent Perry. Tall and thin, with a curiously narrow face and intent unemotional eyes, he

44

seemed the very embodiment of objective observation and deduction, and proceeded to make a series of considered statements.

The dead man, he reported, appeared to be of about the age indicated on the passport, forty-four years, in good health and well-nourished. It was his opinion that the bruise on the chest could not possibly have been caused by the type of fall described by Inspector Diplock. As far as he could tell it had been caused by a violent kick, the imprint of the sharp edge of a shoe sole, probably of some kind of synthetic rubber, being clear almost beyond question. No doubt the Scotland Yard photographer would establish the fact.

There was a temporary interruption while Detective-Constables Boyce and Strickland were given instructions and dispatched to the mortuary.

'I take it that this kick or blow was not the direct cause of death?' Pollard asked, when the discussion was resumed.

Dr Netley folded his hands in the attitude of prayer, and then rested them horizontally on the table in front of him.

'Your conclusion is correct, Superintendent,' he replied in his high brittle voice. 'The immediate cause of death was a severe fracture of the base of the skull, compatible with a backward fall of the type described to me. There were also compatible subsidiary injuries, including a broken neck.'

'Were there any signs of a struggle having taken place?'

'If you refer to a struggle with an assailant, none. A deposit under the fingernails, two of which are broken, suggests that the dead man may have struggled to escape from his confinement. I have taken a sample of this deposit for laboratory analysis.'

Pollard glanced enquiringly at Inspector Diplock, who was looking worried.

'As far as I could ascertain, sir,' he said, 'nobody touched the sliding panel over the entrance to the priest's hole after

Lord Seton helped the American lady to shift it this morning. I thought it was better to leave it till you came down.'

'That's fine,' Pollard told him. 'We'll tackle it as soon as we get out there, and find out how it works from the inside, among other things. Did Peplow try to break his fall, Dr Netley?'

'Judging from the absence of abrasions on the hands, not at all.'

'It looks as though either he was suddenly attacked by someone he trusted, an accomplice, say,' suggested Superintendent Perry, 'or when his reactions were slowed down, by lack of oxygen in the hole, perhaps?'

'Or by whisky,' remarked Major Egerton. 'We found a practically empty flask down there.'

The pathologist was showing signs of restlessness.

'The contents of the stomach and viscera will be analysed,' he said shortly.

'We mustn't detain you, Dr Netley,' Pollard interposed tactfully, 'but before you go, here's the inevitable question. What about the probable time of death?'

As he expected, Dr Netley was extremely reluctant even to hazard an opinion, on the grounds that the temperature conditions in the priest's hole had not yet been established. Finally, he agreed that death was unlikely to have taken place earlier than nine o'clock on the previous evening, or later than five o'clock that morning.

After the pathologist's departure and a brief discussion with the Chief Constable and Superintendent Perry, Pollard went over to the mortuary with Inspector Diplock. Boyce and Strickland had finished their fingerprinting and photography, and Pollard stood looking down on Raymond Peplow's face with interest. It struck him that the immobilisation of death had failed to cancel out a suggestion of daredevilry.

'Any distinguishing marks on the body?' he asked.

'He seems to have taken a few knocks, but there are no operation scars,' Inspector Diplock replied. 'Good teeth.

He's kept the lot, with only a few fillings. Everything he had on him's been listed and put over there. One thing's certain: robbery from the person didn't come into it.'

Pollard fingered the good-quality clothes of foreign make. There was a well-filled wallet, and travellers' cheques to the value of three hundred pounds. A cheque book on a Buenos Aires branch of an Argentine bank was brand new. There was a bunch of keys, and the return half of a first-class rail ticket from London to Crockmouth, issued on the previous day, but no personal papers except the passport. Pollard examined this carefully. It had been issued a year earlier, replacing a previous one. The photograph and personal description tallied with the appearance of the dead man, who had been born in London. His occupation was described as 'realtor'. Turning over the pages Pollard found that Raymond Peplow had visited New York in the previous spring, and entered the UK at Heathrow eight days earlier. It ought not to be too difficult to find out where he had stayed.

'We'd better make tracks for Brent,' he said, looking at his watch. 'It's after eleven already. Lord Seton knows we're coming over tonight, I take it?'

Driving out in the first car with Inspector Diplock, Pollard concentrated on filling in the skeleton biography of *Who's Who*. The eighth Earl took shape as a prominent local figure and a good landlord and employer, but a certain lack of warmth was apparent. Pressed, Inspector Diplock admitted that some thought that Lord Seton was a bit too much of a business man for an earl. Unreasonable for these days, maybe, but that's what they felt. He'd made a good thing out of opening Brent to the public, and was on company boards up in London, too. And his sister, Lady Arminel, was the same with the market garden on the estate.

Pollard noted with amusement that the benevolent father-figure and Lady Bountiful image of the nobility appeared to linger on in Crockmouth minds.

'Lord Seton hasn't a son, has he?'

'No, sir, nor ever will have, unless the Countess came to die, and he took another wife. They can't have any more family. She had a bad illness after the second little girl was born, and there was an operation. Sad for them. A very nice lady, the Countess, and well liked by everyone, for all that she's shy and retiring. A real good-looker, she is.'

'Who's the heir, then?' Pollard asked.

'His lordship's brother, the Honourable Giles Tirle. He's a professor, up at Oxford, and writes books about old houses. He's married, with two boys, and lives at Brent, the same as Lady Arminel does.'

'Good heavens! They're not all one household, surely?'

'Oh, no, sir. Quite separate. When the present Lord Seton came in for the title, he had flats and maisonettes made for them all. Sensible: it's much better for these old places to be lived in. Saves them all money, too, I don't doubt.'

'How long has Brent been open to the public?'

'This is the third summer. They close down for the winter.'

Pollard relapsed into thought, his imagination moving from one aspect to another of this unexpected and unwelcome concentration of family on the scene of the mysterious death of Raymond Peplow. He foresaw with dismay the umbrage-provoking enquiries he would have to make about whereabouts and movements on the previous night. Even more hideous was the prospect of one of these Tirles being involved. Of course, at this social level there would be some resident staff, surely, especially as there seemed to be money around?

The north-western quadrant of the sky was still faintly luminous, and enshrined an evening star of startling brilliance. There was little traffic on the road, and waves of cool air swept in through the open windows of the car, carrying the lingering fragrance of a summer day. They began to slow down, and came to a halt before closed gates, whose supporting pillars were crowned by heraldic beasts looming overhead in the dusk. A uniformed figure stepped into the path of the headlights and saluted. After a brief colloquy with Inspector Diplock he opened the gates, and they drove on into the park, followed by the second car.

'That's Brent,' remarked the Inspector unnecessarily.

Pollard caught his breath at the sight of the house, silver-filigree in the moonlight against a backdrop of night-shrouded hills. Pure theatre, he thought, echoing Maurice Corden of Stately Homes Limited, on his initial visit. The scatter of lighted windows suggested actors poised in the wings for their entrances. . . .

As they drew nearer, the great façade became increasingly dominant, dwarfing the cars to insignificance as they drew up in the forecourt. As they did so the front door opened, letting out a long shaft of light in which another uniformed figure stood silhouetted, a tiny mannikin in a dramatic context.

Pollard followed Inspector Diplock through a screens passage, their footsteps echoing in apparently limitless space. He at once identified the composite smell of an old, inhabited and cared-for house: slowly crumbling stone, wood treated with preservative, furniture polish and flowers. He forced himself to concentrate on the lie of the land. A great oak staircase with a series of half-landings led up to a rather narrow passage. They turned left along this, and he caught glimpses through windows of an inner courtyard on his right. At the end of the passage a door barred further progress, carrying the notice STRICTLY PRIVATE.

'Lord Seton's quarters,' indicated Inspector Diplock. 'This is us.'

He stopped at the last door on the left, examined and broke a seal, and produced a key from his pocket. For a split second Pollard saw a bright rectangle at floor level on the far side of the room now opened to them, an Alice-in-Wonderland entry into the bizarre world where the case had originated. Then switches clicked, and there was a flood of light glancing off carved panelling, and hinting at a host of tiny elegancies behind the glass of showcases.

Inspector Diplock strode forward and stared at the opening, clearing his throat loudly.

'Getting the chap up out of there was a proper picnic,' he remarked.

Pollard lowered himself to the floor, thrusting his head and shoulders through the entrance to the priest's hole. The grim little cavity below, excavated in the immensely thick outer wall of the fifteenth-century house, looked about five feet high and four feet wide. It ran back into shadow, but surely not far? He sniffed the musty air thoughtfully, as he remembered that the sliding panel had been open for the past twelve hours. It seemed impossible that two men could have hidden in so cramped and badly ventilated a space for long. But if Peplow hadn't brought along an accomplice, it was going to look uncomfortably like an inside job. Pollard groaned inwardly as he extricated himself and stood up again.

'Do you happen to know if the door of this room is locked at night?' he asked the Inspector.

'No, it isn't. They don't lock any of the inside doors except the ones leading to the private apartments, and those have keys beside them behind glass. In case of fire, Lord Seton said. But all the windows have shutters and safety catches.'

'So if Peplow had another chap with him, this other fellow could have hidden anywhere in the public rooms. I wonder why Peplow dug in down in that frowsty little bolthole? Once the place had shut for the night he could have come out and found somewhere comfortable.'

'Could have thought there was a night watchman,' suggested Sergeant Toye.

'For anyone planning an important robbery he doesn't seem to have done much homework. Take that rope ladder, for instance. As they don't lock the inside doors, all he'd got to do after lifting the swag was to clear off through a ground floor door or window. I suppose one was found open this morning?'

'This is it,' replied Inspector Diplock. 'I questioned Emmett, the caretaker who locks up at night, and he swore nothing was unfastened when he opened up today. He seemed uneasy, but I couldn't shake him. Reckon he's been fixed. Somebody got away.'

'How long has he been here?'

'Ten years. Must've been satisfactory up to date.'

'There has to be a first time,' Pollard replied. 'We'll have to put him through it tomorrow, but we'd better go along to Lord Seton now. It's after twelve. Strickland and Boyce, you get cracking on this room. The panel and the area round it, of course, and the showcases. Pretty hopeless for dabs, I'm afraid. The whole place will either be smothered in them, or dusted clean yesterday morning. Then go down into the hole, and dredge up anything you can find.'

'Right, sir.' Detective-Constable Strickland removed his coat purposefully.

Pausing in the doorway, Pollard glanced round the room, stifling a sense of sacrilege.

'For God's sake don't muck the place up more than you must.'

'No, sir,' the two young men replied in chorus, the shadow of a wink passing between them.

As Pollard went out he caught a *sotto voce* remark to the effect that the dump was right up the Super's street, and grinned. He followed Inspector Diplock downstairs to the screens, through another door marked STRICTLY PRIVATE, and along a passage immediately below the one leading to the miniatures room. A right-angled turn brought them out into eighteenth-century spaciousness.

'Lord Seton's office,' murmured the Inspector as they halted at a door from beneath which came whimperings and snufflings.

At his thunderous knock a tumult of hysterical barking broke out, through which they heard a shouted summons to come in. As the door opened a tangle of squirming cocker spaniels erupted into the corridor, nosing the men's shoes and scrabbling at their trouser legs. Through a haze of cigar smoke Pollard saw a figure levering itself up from an armchair. The next moment Inspector Diplock was performing inaudible introductions to a good-looking fair man in early middle age, whose innate assurance was oddly at variance with his obvious tension.

'I'm extremely sorry to have kept you up like this, Lord Seton,' Pollard said, the dogs having suddenly subsided. 'I'm afraid there's been a serious development. The post-mortem has established that the man found in the priest's hole didn't die as the result of an accident.'

For a full second Lord Seton stared at him.

'I'm not with you,' he said, a slight edge on his voice. 'You surely can't mean the fellow came here to commit a robbery, and then committed suicide instead?'

'No, I don't,' Pollard replied bluntly. 'He died because someone gave him a kick in the chest which sent him over backwards to fracture the base of his skull. We are, of course, now treating the case as one of manslaughter, or possibly murder.'

'But it simply doesn't make sense.' The remark came out spontaneously, even explosively.

'Make sense?' queried Pollard.

Lord Seton made an abrupt movement, as if repudiating a slip of the tongue.

'Won't you sit down?' He indicated chairs.

'Thank you,' Pollard said. 'Now that Inspector Diplock's handed over to us he's returning to Crockmouth, but I should be grateful for information on one or two points, late though it is.'

'Anything I can tell you, naturally. Can you find your own way out, Diplock?'

Refusing drinks and accepting cigarettes, Pollard took an armchair facing Lord Seton, while Toye faded into the background and took out his notebook. The spaniels relapsed into slumber on the hearthrug.

'I need hardly say that this is a very odd business,' Pollard opened, feeling for his approach. 'At the moment we've very little to go on, except the body. All we can do is to try to get Raymond Peplow into some sort of context. Scotland Yard is dealing with his Argentine connections, and our immediate job is to discover any local links he may have had. I gather from Inspector Diplock that he is quite unknown to you?'

There was a slight sound as Lord Seton's brandy and soda flooded over the small table at his side and began to trickle on to the carpet. He swore briefly, and mopped with a handkerchief, waving aside Toye, who had come forward to help.

'No, don't trouble, thanks. Damn nuisance: it takes the polish off. Sorry, Superintendent. Where were we? No, to my knowledge I've never met Peplow in my life. Isn't it pretty obvious, though, that he's mixed up in these other country house break-ins?'

'It certainly looks likely,' Pollard agreed. 'However, at the moment we're concentrating on his movements down here. I expect you know already that he travelled from London to Crockmouth by train on Tuesday morning or early afternoon, and then somehow got himself out here. In your opinion, could he have joined an escorted tour of the house, given his guide the slip, and managed to go to ground in the priest's hole?'

Lord Seton exhaled a mouthful of smoke before answering.

'Yes, to the first part of your question,' he replied, 'assuming that he'd already got the hang of the place, presumably by having gone round before. But he couldn't have been in the hole until after the last party of the day had gone round. Every party is given the chance of looking down into it.'

'I see,' said Pollard. 'Are there other places where he might have hidden temporarily?'

'I suppose so, if he'd looked slippy, and had luck. He could have dived under a bed with hangings, for instance.'

'What about the mechanics of the sliding panel? Is it tricky to work?'

'Not really. Anyone who had watched one of the guides carefully could probably manage it after a few boss shots. It's only a case of pressing on one particular bit of the carving.'

'Thank you,' Pollard said. 'That clears up another point. Would you tell me now when and how the public rooms are closed for the night?'

'The house closes at half-past five. Emmett, our caretaker and odd-job man, goes round at once, and locks the front and courtyard doors, and the safety catches on the windows. We don't lock the internal doors, apart from those into my own and my brother's parts of the house.'

'So the public rooms are sealed off at night, so to speak?'

'Yes.'

'Does Emmett search them each evening?'

'Well, he takes a look round, of course, in case anyone's hanging about, but I can't say we check up on every hole and corner. Perhaps we should. There must have been two chaps in the place on Tuesday evening, presumably.'

'An accomplice, with whom Peplow later had a row, with disastrous results?' Pollard suggested smoothly. 'Naturally,' he went on, 'we're anxious to find out if anyone noticed Peplow here during the afternoon, with or without a companion. I'm afraid it means interviewing everyone who was on duty here on Tuesday afternoon, and in residence on Tuesday night. Would this include yourself?'

'On Tuesday afternoon I was at a board meeting of Houseware Amalgamated in the City. I got back here at half-past six, and at seven I left by car with my wife and sister-in-law for a public dinner in Fulminster, at which I was speaking.' Lord Seton's tone was cool.

Pollard looked up sharply.

'This is possibly rather important. Was the dinner much publicised? I mean, was it advertised, for instance, that you were among the speakers?'

'To some extent, yes. It was a dinner organised in aid of a National Trust local appeal. I take your point. It had not occurred to me.'

'The most puzzling aspect of the events of Tuesday night,' Pollard said, after a pause, 'is the statement your caretaker made to Inspector Diplock. He says that he found all outer doors and windows in the public sector of the house fastened as usual when he opened up on Wednesday morning. Could anyone have got out without leaving one of them open?'

Lord Seton got abruptly to his feet.

'I suggest that you come and see for yourself.'

It was an eerie progress. They were a small island of light, progressing slowly through the darkness of the great house, their footsteps deadened in the flat airlessness. Lord Seton returned only the briefest of answers to occasional questions. Pollard was finally convinced that no one could possibly have left the area of the public rooms without trace, unless possessing keys, or being helped by a confederate inside. All this would have to be gone into. As they were standing in the hall, the tour completed, the courtyard clock struck with melancholy lingering notes.

'This has been most valuable,' he said. 'Once again, I apologise for keeping you up. As soon as my fingerprint experts are through upstairs we shall be going back to Crockmouth for tonight. I'm afraid I must ask you to keep the house closed again tomorrow.'

'So I had already assumed.'

Desperately worried, Pollard thought, and yet, not desperately scared. It's very odd....

'This is a most wonderful house,' he said on a sudden impulse. 'I hope I shall have a chance of seeing it under happier conditions some day.'

Lord Seton looked astonished. As if, Pollard told his wife afterwards, one of the dogs had stood up on its hind legs and expressed an interest in architecture.

'Yes, er, quite,' he said, and reacted automatically with

a touch of showmanship. 'There's an historically interesting sequence of portraits in here.'

He indicated the walls of the hall.

'My wife,' he added, noticing that Pollard's attention was fixed on a portrait immediately above them. 'A Henry Lamb. Some years ago, of course.'

Pollard gazed at the heart-shaped face, with its lovely wide-set eyes and sensitive mouth. Golden hair, worn long and simply dressed, had trapped the light. The pose of the head was a near miracle, he thought, conveying both receptivity and great diffidence.

He became aware that Lord Seton was showing signs of restiveness.

'A perfectly marvellous bit of painting,' he said.

Upstairs in the miniatures room Strickland and Boyce were packing up their equipment.

'Anything in the priest's hole?' Pollard asked.

'Nothing much, sir,' Strickland told him. 'A few fresh crumbs from the chap's sandwiches. Scraps of mortar, and a few stone chippings, dating back to when they hollowed the place out, from the look of 'em. This was the only bit of luck, for what it's worth.'

He held out two pieces of glass secured together with sellotape. Between them was a single long golden hair.

CHAPTER FIVE

INSPECTOR DIPLOCK had driven off from Brent genuinely thankful to have handed over the case, but feeling unexpectedly flat at suddenly being relieved of responsibility for it. However, Superintendent Pollard had said that he wanted him to go on being in on the job, and he was to meet the Yard team at the station at eight-thirty the next morning.

Speculating as to what the next move would be, he found himself hoping that Crockmouth would manage to keep its end up where the Yard was concerned. Even get a letter of congratulation in the end, which could be discreetly leaked to the local paper. At this point it occurred to him that there was a useful line of enquiry which he could follow up himself without waiting to be asked. How and when had Peplow got out to Brent? If this could be established right away it would save time, and might even lead to an accomplice or a gang being identified. In fact, a nice juicy bit of information to hand the Yard chaps on a plate, first thing tomorrow.

Arriving at his home, Inspector Diplock garaged his car, let himself in, and settled down to hard thinking and the snack left out for him by his wife. As he worked through a stout slab of veal and ham pie he considered the known facts of the case in his careful methodical way. His experience inclined him to believe that the commonsense approach to a problem generally paid off. Peplow could have turned up at Brent any time after the house opened on Tuesday afternoon, hung around unobtrusively, and managed to slip into the priest's hole when everybody else had cleared off. Was it likely, though, that he'd risk being seen around the place a moment longer than was necessary? Unless the caretaker had been fixed, wasn't it much more probable that he'd arrive as late as possible, and nip down the hole when the last visitors had moved on? And one useful piece of information which he, Harry Diplock, had acquired on the previous afternoon was that the last party on Tuesday had been a Blennerhasset coach tour.

He put down his knife and fork with a clatter, pushed the empty plate aside, and poured himself out a glass of beer. He sat on at the kitchen table, breathing heavily through his nose as he invariably did when thinking hard.

If Peplow had gone out in that coach, he obviously hadn't returned to Crockmouth in it. The driver would know if he'd been short of a passenger on the inward journey... Another thing, too. If Peplow had been on board, either he or a confederate must have booked a seat. One of the clerks in Blennerhasset's office might remember something useful. A sensible course of action was opening up nicely. He'd ring Joe Blennerhasset at his home at—say—six-thirty next morning. Even allowing for the inevitable delays you met with in making enquiries, it ought to be possible to have run the coach driver to earth before the meeting with the Yard lot at half-past eight. Feeling braced at the prospect ahead, Inspector Diplock gulped down the rest of the beer, stacked the crocks neatly in the sink, and went upstairs to bed.

Much refreshed by a few hours of sound sleep, he arrived at the police station according to schedule, and punctually at six-thirty dialled the Blennerhassets' number. He was not surprised that no one answered at once. Joe and his missis would be in bed and asleep at this hour, and the phone probably rang downstairs. But as the persistent burr-burr went on and on he became first irritated, and then puzzled. Finally he accepted the all-too-familiar fact that his programme was not working out according to plan, hurried out to his car, and set off for the house, which was tiresomely on the far side of the town.

On arrival he spared a glance for the well-kept garden and immaculate paintwork, and a brief reflection that old Joe had done better than he knew when he sank his war gratuity in a couple of rickety old coaches twenty years back. The curtains of the ground floor rooms were drawn, but he saw to his relief that the bedroom windows were open. He pressed the bell push, and set melodious chimes going. Nothing happened. After two further attempts he grabbed the shining brass knocker and hammered on the front door. Then standing back, he neatly lobbed a small handful of gravel through one of the open windows.

'Anyone up there?' he called loudly.

Next moment the agitated face of a middle-aged woman appeared, surmounted by a frilly pink confection.

'Whatever's the matter?' she demanded. 'Goodness, it's the police. It's not—it's not Joe, is it? Oh, my God!'

'Morning, Mrs Blennerhasset. Not to worry,' Inspector Diplock assured her. 'Sorry to get you out of bed so early, but I want a word with your husband. Something to do with the business. He's not away, is he?' he added, with some dismay.

'Why, it's Inspector Diplock,' she exclaimed. 'I was so fussed I didn't see who it was right away. Yes, he's away, over in Brussels. It's some sort of conference about continental coach tours. We're branching out, you—'

'Who's in charge when he's away?'

'Jack Treadgold, ever since Jim Morris went off to Midland Red. But whatever's wrong? There hasn't been a fire at the garage, has there, and the season just starting?'

'Nothing like that. Treadgold's on the phone, I take it?'

'Oh, yes. He'd have to be. If you don't mind me coming down like this you can use ours if you're in a hurry.'

Assuring Mrs Blennerhasset that he did not mind at all, Inspector Diplock waited with what patience he could muster until he heard her unbolting the front door.

'The phone's here, in this little lobby,' she told him. 'Is

it a break-in at the office?'

Once again he reassured her, while flicking through the pages of the telephone directory, and dialling the Treadgolds' number. A woman's voice came over the line.

'Inspector Diplock here, Mrs Treadgold. Can I have a word with your husband? Nothing to worry about.'

'I'm afraid he's out. Shall I ask him to ring you back?'

'Is he down at the office?'

'No. He's taken the kiddies to the beach for a swim before breakfast.'

Glancing at his watch, Inspector Diplock asked when she expected the party back.

'Oh, any time now. I've got to get the kiddies off to school, you see.'

'I'll be over right away,' he told her firmly, putting down the receiver.

He drove as fast as he dared through the town to a rather less affluent suburb on the far side. An estate car stood outside the Treadgolds' house, a hopeful sign that the bathers had returned. He arrived at the front door to find it open, and a wide-eyed blonde struggling to explain something to a dark man in bathing trunks. Three damp and sandy children goggled at the sight of a policeman on the doorstep. Mr Treadgold turned and caught sight of him.

'Here, buzz off and get dressed,' he adjured his offspring. 'Come in, Inspector, and tell me the worst. Fire, or a break-in? It would happen when the boss is away living it up in Brussels.'

Explaining once again that no disaster of any kind had befallen Blennerhasset's, Inspector Diplock briefly outlined the object of his visit.

'If that's all you want, I can tell you here and now,' Mr Treadgold replied. 'A chap called Syd Bradford took out that coach. During the season we have a stand-by rota for extra tours, and I briefed him myself on Tuesday morning, when I saw we'd need to put another coach on. He's one of our older drivers. Reliable chap.'

'I suppose you don't know his address offhand?'

'Afraid not. Tell you what, though. Let me get a shirt and some trousers on, and we'll run down to the office for it.'

Within a few minutes the two cars were making for the centre of Crockmouth. On arriving at the office on the Esplanade, they found the doors open, and a cleaner mopping the floor. She stared at them, open-mouthed.

'OK, love,' Mr Treadgold assured her, with a grin and a wave of his hand. 'The Inspector hasn't come for you this time.'

In the manager's office he quickly thumbed through a card-index.

'Adams ... Best ... Bradford, S. H. Here we are. 17, Summerlawn Road. You know it, I expect?'

'I do,' replied Inspector Diplock grimly. 'It's right out on the Fulminster road. Council estate. Thanks for your help over this, Mr Treadgold. As I said, I'll have to bother you again, I'm afraid, over the booking of the chap's seat on the coach.'

'OK by me, Inspector. Glad to be on the right side of the law. I hope you find Syd Bradford at his place, by the way. It's his day off, and he likes to go off early in his boat. Keen fisherman, our Syd.'

Feeling that this eventuality would really be the last straw, Inspector Diplock took to the road once again, mentally reviewing the possibility of pursuing his quarry out to sea in a commandeered motorboat. On reaching the estate he heartily cursed the Council for their idiocy in giving all the roads virtually identical names, such as Summerhay, Summerlea and Summerdown. At last he arrived at 17, Summerlawn Road.

The door was opened in answer to his knock by a large stolid man with grizzled hair and an impassive face. He took in his caller, and proceeded to block the entrance to his home by leaning against one door jamb, and propping a massive arm against the other.

'Mr Sydney Bradford?' enquired Inspector Diplock.

The man admitted cautiously that this was his name.

'You're a driver for Blennerhasset's, aren't you? I understand from Mr Treadgold that you took out a late coach to Brent last Tuesday. Correct?'

'Correct. And no incidents nor complaints, what's more.'

'No one said there were. All I want to know is whether you brought back the same number of passengers that you took out?'

A flicker of interest manifested itself in Syd Bradford's eyes.

'One less on the inward journey. Gent sent a message to say he'd met friends an' was going back in their car, see?'

A thrill of triumph went through Inspector Diplock.

'Thanks, Mr Bradford,' he said. 'You've heard what happened at Brent on Tuesday night, I expect. You may be an important witness. The Scotland Yard Superintendent'll want to see you. Come along to the station by half-past eight, will you?'

'OK,' replied Syd Bradford, almost with alacrity.

Inspector Diplock turned his car, and headed for the police station and a telephone.

Although his night's sleep had been even shorter than Inspector Diplock's, Pollard woke at an early hour on Thursday morning. Simultaneously with the return of consciousness came a pang at the realisation of Jane's absence. Then the case crowded into his mind to the exclusion of all else.

His thoughts moved in a dissatisfied way from Lord Seton's puzzling reactions, to Emmett, as yet only a name, but certainly a potential suspect as far as collaboration with Peplow went. Then they moved on to Peplow's hypothetical accomplice, that convenient but unconvincing figure with a decided touch of burlesque about him. What the hell did Peplow want with an accomplice, anyway? He'd got all the necessary gear on him for opening showcases.

He must have been after the miniatures, because the rope ladder showed that he had expected to be locked inside the room. The whole collection could have been carried off in his rucksack and pockets. No need for a helper on that score.

Then there was the golden hair caught on the rough stone wall of the hole. Pollard tried to square the athleticism needed for the descent into the latter with the impression of Lady Seton he had formed from her portrait. Could there have been a variation on the Macbeth theme, he wondered? Suppose Lord Seton had heard a suspicious noise in the miniatures room, gone to investigate, been threatened by the emergent Peplow with a gun, and in trying to kick the weapon from his hand, had sent him over backwards down the steps. Enter Lady Seton, transformed by the crisis into a woman of steel. She climbs down into the priest's hole to make sure that the man is dead, catching her flowing hair on the wall. Returning to her husband, she insists on concealment. . . .

Pollard rolled over with an impatient snort, and realised that he was extremely hungry. A glance at his watch showed him that it was still only half-past six. Why on earth couldn't English hotels start serving breakfast a bit earlier? They managed a damn sight better . . .

He was coming downstairs before it was fully light in a small hotel in the Bernese Oberland, and picking his way through the rucksacks, ice axes and coils of rope which littered the hall. In the dining room, which smelt gorgeously of coffee, the usual types were knocking back hunks of bread and cherry jam. No one spoke. They'd all...got...their...minds...on...getting...off...

He jerked back into consciousness once more to find that it was twenty minutes to eight, and leapt hastily out of bed. As he went automatically through the routine of shaving, bathing and dressing, his thoughts oscillated unproductively as before. Completing his toilet in record time he hurried down to the hotel dining room. Toye was already installed, and studying the menu. Pollard learnt that Boyce and Strickland had breakfasted, and gone on ahead to the police station to do their stuff with last night's dabs.

'What's your morning-after reaction to Lord Seton?' he asked, when they had given their orders.

'He's mixed up in it all right,' replied Toye decisively. 'Rattled good and proper last night, wasn't he?'

'You can be rattled because you've got the wind up, or because you're worried. He struck me as worried rather than windy.'

Toye looked puzzled.

'I'm not with you, sir. Surely a chap who's scared *is* worried?'

'Let's put it another way. Can you see Lord Seton doing Peplow, probably accidentally or in self-defence, and then being such a b.f. as to try and cover it up?'

Toye contemplated the plate of porridge which had been put in front of him.

'No, I can't, and that's a fact,' he said at last. 'I can see him going for an intruder, and lamming him too hard by mistake, but not being so daft as not to report it. Knows his way round too well, I'd say.'

'My opinion exactly. What's he worried about, then? Loss of takings while the place is closed? Not him. He knows well enough that the publicity will bring people swarming like ants when he opens again. Yes?' he added, turning to a waiter.

'You're wanted on the telephone, sir. First right, and first left. Incoming calls box.'

Thrusting back his chair, Pollard departed. A few minutes later he returned with the vestiges of a grin on his face.

'Diplock,' he said, sitting down again. 'Elaborately casual, to hide the fact that he's bursting with pride at the local boys getting a beat ahead. He's found the driver of the last coach party at Brent on Tuesday afternoon, and the chap says one of the passengers sent a message at the last minute to say he was going back in a friend's car.'

'Mayn't be anything to do with Peplow,' Toye commented cautiously.

'Of course it mayn't. On the other hand it may. Cheery chap this morning, aren't you? If we don't get a bit of luck in this case, the outlook's anything but hopeful. It was a damn good effort on Diplock's part. I hope I sounded impressed enough. He's gone off to the coach people's office now, to see if he can pick up anything about the booking of Peplow's seat.'

There was a brief interval during which both men concentrated on their bacon and eggs.

'That hair,' Pollard said presently. 'I don't believe it's one of Lady Seton's. I saw her portrait last night. She's definitely not the type to climb in and out of hiding holes.'

Toye looked scandalised.

'Can't tell from a picture, surely, can you? The chaps that paint 'em have to pretty you up, or they'd be out of a job.'

'Good portrait painters can't help telling the truth about their sitters. Sometimes it's very awkward, I can tell you. You ought to hear my wife on the subject. However, we'll be seeing her ladyship for ourselves this morning. More coffee?'

Toye accepted a second cup, and carefully spread marmalade on another piece of toast.

'I've been through the notes,' he said. 'What I can't make out is what Peplow wanted with an accomplice. It seems the most likely explanation that he'd brought somebody along, and it ended up in a row and him getting kicked down the steps, but what was the point of having a second chap there? Double risk, and nothing gained that I can figure out.'

'There I'm absolutely with you,' Pollard replied. 'In fact, the sheer improbability of its being the explanation is on my mind. I don't like the implications one bit. Finished eating? We'd better push along.'

A quarter of an hour later, as Pollard and Toye walked into the police station they found that the case had suddenly gathered momentum. Pollard was hurriedly summoned to the telephone to take a call from the Yard which was just coming through.

'Get everything you can out of the driver,' he said to Toye over his shoulder. 'I may be tied up for some time.'

Syd Bradford had already arrived, and was waiting with an expression of patient cynicism designed to cover a pleasurable sense of importance. After providing the usual particulars about himself, he stated that Tuesday's Panoramic Extra had gone much as usual until passengers began boarding the coach in the car park at Brent, about ten to six. A chap had come up to him, and brought a message to say that another gent had met up with a friend who'd come by car, and was going back with him.

'Considerate,' Syd Bradford allowed. 'A lot of 'em wouldn't trouble themselves.'

'So you were one down on the run home?' asked Toye.

'Ain't that what I'm saying? We went out thirty-nine, an' came back thirty-eight. Forty-two seater, it was.'

'Can you remember what the chap who brought the message was like?'

'Smallish bloke, going bald on top. Excitable type, sayin' the same thing ten times over. Visitor, for sure. He'd got a whackin' great camera and what-have-you slung round him. I didn't take much notice. Too busy countin' 'eads.'

'Can you remember anything about the passenger who dropped out?'

Syd Bradford made it clear that he considered the question unreasonable. He drove hundreds every week in the holiday season. His job was taking 'em places, and bringin' 'em back in one piece, and it took some doing, the way some of 'em went on.

' 'E wasn't a black, or a Chinese, or a noodist,' he added with heavy sarcasm. 'I'll go that far, but—'

His protest was abruptly cut short by the arrival of

66

Inspector Diplock with the light of triumph in his eye.

'Nobody at Blennerhasset's can remember Peplow coming in to book,' he said, 'or any single booking, for that matter. You'd hardly expect it at this time of year, with so many visitors around. But we've got the chap who says he was asked to give the driver the message. One of the clerks remembered a party of six or seven coming in to book for the trip, and one of them saying they were from the Cliffside Hotel. We struck lucky there right away. It's a Mr Leonard Cudwinkle. He's outside in the office. Will you have him in?'

'You Crockmouth chaps cover the ground,' replied Toye. 'Yeah, let's have him meet up with Mr Bradford here.'

Inspector Diplock went out looking gratified, and a couple of moments later ushered in the smallish balding holidaymaker of Syd Bradford's description, who was accorded a grudging recognition by the latter. He was carrying a large camera and other photographic impedimenta, and at once embarked on an unsolicited statement.

Cutting him short, Toye politely thanked Syd Bradford for his assistance, and escorted him out.

'Now, Mr Cudwinkle,' he said briskly as he returned, 'we needn't keep you long. You won't want to waste your holiday in here. Just a few facts about yourself first, please. Your full name and address?'

Looking as crestfallen as a disappointed child, Mr Cudwinkle provided these and other particulars.

'That's fine,' said Toye, noting them down. 'Now, we understand that a fellow passenger on the coach tour to Brent last Tuesday asked you to tell the driver that he was returning with friends. Correct?'

Mr Cudwinkle agreed that this had been the case, and began to enlarge on the circumstances under which the request had been made. In his opinion the tour of the house had been a bit of a washout. For all that it was her own home, the lady who took them round hadn't seemed sure of herself. Not what you'd call convincing. Why, when she was talking about the pictures some of the party got bored, and went back the way they'd come, to take a look at the courtyard, someone in the coach told him on the way home.

Pressed on this point he was emphatic that he had seen a few people going back into the screens passage, but was unable to say if the man who spoke to him about not returning with the party was one of them.

'When exactly did this chap come up and speak to you?' Toye asked.

'While we were waiting to go up the stairs. The crush was terrible, simply terrible,' Mr Cudwinkle assured him volubly. 'We'd joined on to the first half of our lot, and were all waiting together, and at the same time a crowd of Boy Scouts were making their way down. Not at all well managed. In the coach going back—'

'Where were you standing when the man spoke to you?' persisted Toye.

'Right at the back. I'd stayed behind to photograph an Adam fireplace. I needn't have hurried, either. There everybody was, stuck at the bottom of the stairs—'

'Had you ever seen the man before?'

'Not that I remember, and I've got an eye for a face, Sergeant. If I ever had—'

'Can you describe him?'

Mr Cudwinkle took a deep breath, and was away. Photography was the big thing in his life, he explained. Actually, he was the secretary of the Central Counties Camera Club, the largest of its kind in the country. Every man, woman and child he met was a possible portrait study to him. He had noticed at once that the gentleman who asked him to give the message had a well-shaped head.

'From what I saw of the house last night, the light wasn't any too good,' Toye interrupted. 'I don't suppose you saw him very clearly, did you?'

Nettled, Mr Cudwinkle gave a surprisingly accurate description of Raymond Peplow, going on from his features, colouring and build to his clothes, and finally to his camera.

'That's when I realised there was something odd about him,' he concluded breathlessly.

Toye looked up sharply.

'Odd?'

'Well, look at his clothes. Cost a packet. Casuals, if you like, but that little lot never came off a Marks and Sparks peg. Expensive foreign cut—you can't mistake it, not if you've got an eye for a picture. Now, I ask you, would a chap who was keen enough on photography to tote a camera around, and could afford clothes like that, have been content with a ropey old discontinued Kodak model? Course he wouldn't. Must have been a blind.'

Pollard allowed that Mr Cudwinkle had a point there. He felt disposed to take him rather more seriously.

'Did you see this chap again after he asked you to take the message?'

'No, I didn't. Just then we started moving at last, and I was dead keen on getting upstairs. They've got some wonderful ceilings—work of local craftsmen—I wanted to—'

'I must ask you to come with me to the mortuary now,' Toye broke in, 'and see if you can identify the body as that of the man we've been talking about. It will only take a few minutes.'

To Toye's disgust, eager gratification spread over Mr Cudwinkle's face, and he leapt to his feet. Reflecting distastefully on human nature, Toye led the way in silence.

'That's him,' Mr Cudwinkle said categorically, after a prolonged scrutiny of Raymond Peplow's remains. 'I'll swear to it.'

'Right,' replied Toye, replacing the sheet. 'Now, if you'll come back to the station—'

Darting over to the pile of the deceased's clothing and other belongings, Mr Cudwinkle had seized the Kodak, and, holding it up, launched out on a string of technicalities. On being firmly interrupted by Toye, he suddenly became a pleading small boy, his eyes alight with enthusiasm.

'No objection, is there?' he asked anxiously, now grabbing his own camera. He jerked his head in the direction of the sheeted figure. 'Just a coupla flash shots. It's the Club's summer competition, y'know. One of the set subjects is "The End of the Road". You just couldn't beat this for an original interpretation. There's a special class for originality.'

Outraged, Toye curtly informed him that unauthorised photography in the mortuary would be a breach of regulations, and hustled him out. Shortly afterwards, having secured his signature to a cut-and-dried statement, he saw him off the premises and went in search of Pollard, whom he found writing up his notes.

'Peplow went out on that Blennerhasset coach trip all right,' Toye told him, and elaborated.

Pollard threw down his pen and clasped his hands behind his head.

'That's one bit of definite evidence to go on, anyway. What's just come through makes the whole business more crackpot than ever. First of all, the Yard. Peplow's dabs aren't in Records, and they've never heard of him. They're trying to track him down at Somerset House, and doing a check on the high-class robbery boys for a possible link. Longman's working on his trail from Heathrow last week. And Interpol's checking round, but nothing's come along from them yet.'

He broke off to light a cigarette.

'Anything from the Argentine people?' asked Toye.

'Yeah. I'm just coming to that. Their police and the British Consulate say Peplow turned up out there in '37, and has lived there ever since. Didn't even come over for the war. He's never been back as far as anyone knows until he gave out about a couple of weeks ago that he was making a business trip to London.'

'What about his passport?'

'He had a valid British passport when he first went out

there, and has had it renewed by the Consul each time it ran out. No difficulty there.'

'What's he been living on? Has he got a record?'

'No criminal record, barring getting mixed up a few times in brawls down-town in the early days. They say he lived pretty rough at first, taking any job he could get. Then he seems to have got a bit of money together, gone into real estate, and done quite well for himself. No known criminal contacts or dicey political entanglements, and his affairs with women seem to be all very temporary and casual.'

Toye sat staring at Pollard, unwinking as an owl behind his horn-rims.

'But can they know for sure he's never been back here? He can't suddenly have decided to come over and try his hand at a break-in, just out of the blue. It doesn't make sense.'

'Echoes of Lord Seton last night. I've got an idea those words are going to be a sort of theme song running through the whole bloody case. No, of course they can't know for sure. Peplow's made trips to the States like that one last spring. It was perfectly above board on the face of it: an American firm negotiating for a factory site in Buenos Aires, but it could easily have been cover for something criminal. He could have nipped across here on a faked passport, too. The Yard's asked the F.B.I. to make enquiries, but it's a forlorn hope after all this time.'

There was a pause. Pollard doodled absently on a piece of blotting paper.

'In some ways,' he resumed, 'the gen about the chap himself from the Consul is the most interesting thing. Peplow seems to have been a bit of a lone wolf, although an accepted member of the British colony in B.A. Not what you'd call popular: keener on trips into the wilds than the cocktail round, and cagey about his affairs. But occasionally he'd whoop it up, and splash a terrific party which usually ended in people doing the craziest things, just for the hell of it. A latent reckless streak, the Consul called it. Ties up with this Brent business and its fancy touches.'

Toye gave a slight sniff.

'If Peplow was in on an art treasures racket,' he said, in the tone of one determined to stick to down-to-earth probabilities, 'why Brent, for heaven's sake? You'd think he'd have aimed a bit higher, coming all that way.'

Pollard completed his doodle.

'Not necessarily. That sort of market functions on supply and demand, like any other. Brent's got a fine collection of miniatures which aren't for sale. Somebody with plenty of lolly and no scruples could be building up a secret collection to gloat over, and particularly fancy the Charles the Second one. I don't think it need follow that Peplow had a local contact, more's the pity.'

Toye asked if Strickland had pulled anything off with the dabs.

'Peplow's are on the outside of the panel in the right position for opening the thing. Looks as though he must have been down here last week, doesn't it?'

'Didn't he wear gloves?'

'No. Staggering, isn't it? He must have been completely confident, or incredibly slapdash. But the interesting thing is that whoever shut the panel on him went at it like a bull at a gate, and was wearing gloves—rubber ones. And the same glove prints are on the showcase with the royal miniature in it.'

Toye whistled under his breath.

'Peplow's accomplice bobbing up again?' he asked.

'Or Lord Seton, realising that Peplow's a goner, slams the panel after fetching a pair of rubber gloves, and checks up on the showcase.'

'Leaving the American visitors or somebody going round the house to find the body?'

'This is it. Can you see him deliberately fixing it so that a woman guest to his house would almost certainly be bound to discover it? A pretty damnable thing to do to any woman. After all, he's the eighth Earl.'

Toye nodded slowly in agreement.

'It hadn't struck me that way, sir, but you've got something there.'

Pollard looked at his watch.

'Time we made tracks for Brent. Get the car, will you, while I throw a few scraps to the Press boys. I gather they've massed outside.'

A small crowd of newsmen surged forward as Pollard came out, their cameras at the ready. There was a babel of demands for information and protests at continued exclusion from Brent. When would the police ban be lifted?

'When we're through with the place,' Pollard told them. 'Be your age, chaps. What chance would we have of picking up anything useful after you lot had milled through it?'

'Aw, hell,' exclaimed disgusted voices. 'We wanna picture with the spot marked X. That's what the public wants. Be a sport, Super.'

'Let me have one of those guide books, and I'll mark X for you myself, if that's all you want.'

'All we want!' shouted an indignant chorus. A fusillade of questions broke out.

'Who's this guy Peplow, anyway?'

'What's this guff about a royal miniature?'

'Why didn't they find the body till midday yesterday?'

'Who's the American dame who spotted it down the hole? . . .'

'Give me a chance to make myself heard,' Pollard said, 'and I'll tell you what I know. And damn little it is at this stage.'

They subsided, scribbling madly as he reiterated the bare facts and added a few picturesque but unimportant details about the priest's hole and Peplow's equipment. He went on to emphasize the absence of the Setons and Mrs Giles Tirle at a public dinner on Tuesday evening.

'What price the Earl's brother being in the States?' someone asked suggestively,

'America keeps popping up in this business, wouldn't you say?' tried someone else.

'I wouldn't personally,' replied Pollard, 'but then I didn't miss out on geography at school. The Argentine's quite a way from the States.'

This raised a laugh. He made a swift mental note to enquire immediately into the activities of Giles Tirle.

'Cut-throat competition, this Stately Homes racket,' came a voice from the back row. 'What are your views on advertising stunts by the owners?'

'I haven't any. If anyone's interested, the chap who actually spoke to Peplow, and took his message to the coach driver is staying at the Cliffside Hotel.'

The newsmen dispersed enthusiastically and collectively. Just like a shoal of fish in an aquarium tank, moving in perfect unison, Pollard thought. The car came round from the back of the police station, and he got in beside Toye.

They were admitted to Brent by a woman in an overall, who looked at them uneasily, and escorted them to Peggy Blackmore's office without speaking. Uncertain about how to announce them, she flung the door wide and flattened herself against it.

Peggy Blackmore got up quickly from a desk littered with papers. A buxom fifty with a mop of naturally curly hair, she tended to become dishevelled when under stress. Her face was shiny, and she had a crumpled appearance.

'I'm afraid Lord Seton isn't in his office yet,' she told Pollard when he had introduced Toye and himself. 'He rang through just now to say he'd be in by eleven unless the—unless you wanted to see him before then.'

'Eleven will be quite soon enough,' Pollard told her. 'I'm afraid it was very late when we left here last night. You know, I expect, that there had been a fresh development?'

She nodded.

'It's all so awful,' she said shakily. 'Like a nightmare you can't wake up from. If you only knew how Lord Seton and all of them have worked to make opening the house a success, and now this happens ... Is there anything I can do for you at the moment?'

Pollard explained that he had come to examine the public rooms for further traces of anyone having hidden there, and to talk to everyone who had been on duty or slept at Brent on Tuesday.

'As you're free just now,' he said, 'may I start with you? Are you about when the visitors are here?'

Peggy Blackmore shook her head.

'I don't take parties round. I'm working in here during the afternoons.'

'All the same,' Pollard said, 'I'd like you to have a look at the dead man's photograph, and the description of the clothes he was wearing. We know that he came out here on the second Blennerhasset coach, and think he probably paid an earlier visit last week.'

She gave both documents careful attention, but shook her head decisively.

'I'm as sure as one ever can be that I've never seen that man in my life. You don't even know what the other one looked like, I suppose? The one who killed him, and escaped afterwards, I mean?'

'Not yet,' Pollard replied truthfully. He glanced at his watch. 'We'll be back at eleven, then, to see Lord Seton. Thank you for being so helpful.'

As he retraced his steps in the direction of the screens, followed by Toye, he reflected gloomily that the gist of the conversation about Peplow which he had just had was likely to be repeated *ad nauseam* in the course of the day. He stopped at the foot of the magnificent late-sixteenth-century staircase.

'Put in by the Elizabethan builders when they inserted the first floor,' he remarked. 'I'd like to have seen the hall as it originally was. ... Now then, a mob of scouts is blocking the staircase, and the Blennerhassets are jammed in this passage, waiting to go up. The passage, I think, runs back to where you turn left into the eighteenth-century wing, as on the other side. Yes, here we go. Cudwinkle would have been photographing an Adam fireplace in one of these rooms. There's a splendid specimen in here, see? He comes out again with his camera and gadgets, and Peplow, who must have been at the back of the queue, asks him to give the coach driver the message. The next moment the queue starts moving, taking Cudwinkle along with it. What does Peplow do? I rather think he goes back on his tracks, having realised that his party is the last of the day, and no one will be following on.'

Opening a door on the right of the passage Pollard walked into the hall, and came to a standstill. Bridget Seton was standing on the hearth, against the background of a great mass of delphiniums mounting up like blue flames. She was wearing a plain white frock, and holding a single spike in her hand. Inevitably a composite memory of the virgin martyrs of Renaissance painters flashed into his mind, only to be discarded as he came towards her. There was no rapturous expectancy in her lovely face, only withdrawal and a hint of sadness.

'I do apologise, Lady Seton,' he said. 'I had no idea you were in here. May I introduce myself? Detective-Superintendent Pollard of New Scotland Yard, and this is Detective-Sergeant Toye, who is working with me.'

She greeted them both courteously.

'Please don't apologise. Am I in your way? My husband told me you would be here today, and what a terrible situation we have to face.'

'On the contrary,' Pollard told her, 'we should be glad of your help. That newel stairway over there: is it blocked, or a possible way up to the gallery?'

'Yes, it's perfectly usable, but we cord it off in case of an accident to a visitor.'

'If I remember rightly, there's a NO WAY notice on the outside of the gallery door upstairs. Does that mean it isn't locked?'

'Yes. We don't lock it in case of fire, but try to keep

visitors out, as a child could easily fall over the balustrade. Do you think—?'

She broke off and looked at him unhappily.

'Yes,' he said. 'I think that is probably the route by which the man got to the priest's hole without being seen. Will you excuse me a moment?'

After sending Toye to bring in Strickland and Boyce to investigate the newel stairway, he returned.

'Would this be a convenient time for you to spare me a few minutes?' he asked.

'Perfectly convenient. Shall we sit here?'

She slipped red cords from a pair of Chippendale chairs. Pollard eyed them anxiously.

'I'm a fair weight,' he said. 'Is it an undue risk?'

'I don't think so.' She smiled at him.

Waiting for her to be seated he moved the second chair slightly to see her full-face, wondering why her beauty was so disconcerting. Sitting down himself, he told her what was known about Raymond Peplow's movements on Tuesday. As he finished she began to twist her hands restlessly.

'This awful business is simply the result of my being so incompetent as a guide,' she said miserably. 'Any of the others would have noticed that the man was missing at the end of the tour. I'm not a regular guide, you see: I'm so hopeless at it. I'm only called on in an emergency.'

'I don't think you quite appreciate all the facts, Lady Seton,' Pollard told her. 'Peplow came down from London with the clear intention of carrying out a robbery here. He brought housebreaking tools, and food and whisky, and even an air cushion, which suggests that he had decided on the priest's hole from the start. The message to the coach driver ensured that if he was missed by the guide it would be assumed that he had joined his friends. The fact that a less experienced guide took him round was neither here nor there.'

To his surprise he realised that she was unwilling to be absolved from responsibility, and speculated as to why she should nurse a guilt complex. He suddenly remembered Diplock's remarks about the lack of a direct heir. Brent's an extraordinarily dominating place, he thought. I suppose she feels she's failed it.

Faint sounds and a couple of flashes came from the far end of the hall.

'I've just remembered,' Bridget Seton said anxiously. 'There was a man who looked as though he was going to step over the red cord and go up. I called out to him, and he stopped.'

'Can you remember what he looked like?' Pollard asked.

'He was tall and thin, with a very noticeable Adam's apple, and kept on asking questions.'

'Then he certainly wasn't Raymond Peplow,' he said cheerfully. 'I'd like you to look at this photograph and description, and see if it recalls anyone in your party.'

After a careful examination she handed them back.

'No,' she said. 'I've absolutely no recollection of ever having seen this man. But I go quite blank when I'm faced with a lot of people to take round. He could perfectly well have been in my party.'

Pollard passed on to the later part of Tuesday.

'I know that you and your husband and sister-in-law were out for the greater part of the evening,' he said. 'Do you happen to know who was at home?'

'Emmett certainly was. As we were going to be out late he said he would have a look round outside before going to bed. Sometimes in the summer we get hooligans out here from Crockmouth in the evenings. Emmett's wife and daughter were at home, as far as I know, and my husband's sister, Lady Arminel Tirle.'

'How about dogs?' Pollard asked. 'I met your spaniels last night. They were in the house, I expect?'

'Yes, with my daughters' ex-nanny, Mrs Pringle. I'm so sorry, I forgot to mention her. She is one of our resident staff. The Emmetts have a bull terrier, and Lady Arminel has a dachshund.'

'Thank you.' Pollard made a note. 'I've nearly finished these tedious questions. Can you remember at what time you got home from Fulminster?'

'I can remember exactly, as it happens. We remarked on how late it was: ten minutes to twelve.'

'You went to bed as soon as you got in, I expect?'

'My husband did. I had a hot bath first. I find it helps me to get off to sleep after a busy day.'

Pollard's pen checked.

'Were you up and about for long, Lady Seton? I'm asking you this just in case you noticed anything suspicious without realising its importance at the time.'

To his astonishment she looked quite guilty.

'I was, rather. I dozed off in my bath. It's a bad habit of mine which worries my husband, but fortunately he was asleep when I eventually got back to our bedroom. It was nearly one o'clock. But I'm quite sure I didn't notice anything in the least unusual.'

Pollard saw that he must visit the first floor of the Setons' private wing and see the lie of the land.

'Would it be convenient for me to see Mrs Pringle?' he asked.

'Certainly. Shall we go and find her now?'

He delayed deliberately, turning over the pages of his notebook.

'May I just see if there's anything else that I want to ask you?'

Toye and the others had gone out quietly some minutes earlier. The great hall was very still.

'Lady Seton,' he said, looking up at her suddenly, 'when did you last go down into the priest's hole?'

She made a quick movement of revulsion.

'That horrible place? I've never been in it in my life.'

CHAPTER SIX

POLLARD found Mrs Pringle cagey, and realised that she was having difficulty in squaring him with her image of a policeman. Moreover, their surroundings were inhibiting. Lady Seton had installed them in the privacy of the dining room, and they sat formally at one end of the highly-polished table, the other end of which was laid for lunch. Mrs Pringle, diminutive and birdlike, kept darting glances at him. When not actually speaking she kept her lips firmly closed.

Patiently Pollard extracted the information that she had a bed-sitting-room on the first floor, but preferred to sit in the kitchen when her employers were out for the evening, as it was handier for the telephone.

'Did you take any calls on Tuesday evening?' he asked.

'Only one.' Reluctantly she capitulated under his steady interrogative gaze. 'Sir James Mallaby rang about the time he was bringing the American lady and gentleman over. Except for a wrong number,' she added grudgingly.

'A wrong number? That's a well-known dodge of criminals to find out if a house is empty, you know', Pollard told her.

Mrs Pringle looked startled, and then relieved.

'It was somebody wanting Mrs Giles. It often happens. The numbers are the same except for the last figure. You can hear her phone across the courtyard when the windows are open. It rang straight away.'

'It might also have been somebody checking up on that part of the house, mightn't it? You may have told something very important by mentioning these calls, Mrs

Pringle', he went on, playing up to her. 'I'm sure you realise that it mustn't be mentioned to anyone else at present.'

She bridled slightly.

'I'm not one for talking.'

'I'm quite sure you're not. What time was this wrong number call?'

Her small face puckered with concentration.

'Just after half-past nine, it was, when Sir James rang. I always put the time on the pad. I'd hardly sat down when the phone went again. Say twenty to ten.'

Pollard made a note.

'You had the dogs with you, I understand? From what I saw of them last night they seem good watchdogs. Did they bark at all during the evening?'

'I won't stand for their hullabaloo, and they know it', replied Mrs Pringle briskly. 'Snowball—that's Mr Emmett's dog—began to bark about half-past ten, and they must join in, of course, but I soon put a stop to that. I expect that heathenish Siamese cat of Mrs Giles's jumped up on the Emmetts' window ledge, and set him off.'

'Did you let the spaniels out for a run before you went to bed?'

'No, sir.' There was a fractional pause between the two words. 'His lordship sees to that when he comes in. When I went up just on eleven they settled on the mat inside the front door, and not a sound till the car came back.'

'Did you hear anything in the least unusual during the night?'

'Nothing, sir, and I'm a light sleeper.'

Pollard made another note.

'I don't want to bother Lady Seton any further,' he said. 'I wonder if you would take me round this wing of the house? I'd like to see how far it can be watched from the passage outside the miniatures room, among other things.'

Mrs Pringle rose promptly and led the way. Although he examined the lock of the front door with care, Pollard's main objective on the ground floor was the kitchen. On entering it he glanced at the sink and saw the pair of rubber gloves he had half expected to find. After standing at the window and contemplating the back of the Elizabethan house for a few moments he turned to her.

'I want to try a little experiment. Would you sit just where you did on Tuesday evening? Thank you, that's fine. Now just pretend you hear the telephone ringing. Go and answer it, and imagine it's that wrong number call. Deal with it exactly as you did then, and come straight back. All right?'

Looking mystified, she darted off. Pollard took some quick strides over to the sink, pocketed the rubber gloves, and returned to his former position. Mrs Pringle reappeared to find him studying his watch.

'Thank you,' he said, making an entry in his notebook. 'Now, may we go up to the first floor?'

Having arrived there he concentrated on the lie of the land. The Setons' bedroom was in the eighteenth-century part of their private wing, facing west. Immediately opposite, a room which overlooked the courtyard had been subdivided to make a dressing room for Lord Seton, with a bathroom on its north side. Emerging from the dressing room and turning left, one arrived at the locked door into the public part of the house, which Inspector Diplock had pointed out to him the night before.

From the dressing room window he looked across to the open window of the passage outside the miniatures room, and through it to the closed door of the latter. But surely the dressing room curtains would have been drawn late on Tuesday night? On the other hand, the windows would probably have been open, and Lord Seton's attention possibly aroused by some sound. One thing was clear enough. He could have gone through to the miniatures room without passing the bathroom. The corridor was well carpeted. His wife, relaxed and somnolent in her bath, need not have heard a sound.

'I suppose Lady Seton's daughters are still away at school?' he asked for the sake of making conversation, as he followed Mrs Pringle out of the dressing room.

'Lady Amanda is, sir. She's only fifteen. Lady Caroline's been learning French in a family. She's rising eighteen. Coming home this evening, and her bed not made up yet with all this dreadful upset.'

'I won't keep you any longer,' he said. 'Thank you for all your help. Now I want to go back to the hall.'

'We'll have to go down to the ground floor, to get through to the old house: I haven't a key for the door here.'

She escorted him to the screens passage. When he turned to say goodbye Pollard saw that her face was flushed, apparently with indignation.

'It's shameful, such a thing to happen here, in her ladyship's house,' she burst out angrily. 'Let rag, tag and bobtail come in, tramping all over the place, and see what comes of it. It never should've been.'

She shot off so abruptly that Pollard was left to speculate as to whether she was referring to Raymond Peplow's demise or the opening of Brent to the public. He rather thought the latter. Heavy footsteps on the main staircase announced the reappearance of Toye, Strickland, and Boyce, and the team repaired briefly to the car in the forecourt.

'I nicked these from the kitchen sink,' Pollard said, producing a pair of bright blue rubber gloves. 'Any tie-up with the dabs on the panel and show case?'

Strickland pounced, but immediately shook his head.

'Different type, sir. These are Grabtites. It's a popular brand for washing up—my wife has 'em. See the little raised studs to improve the grip? The dabs were made by thin gloves with a smooth surface. Got that blow-up you did, Boyce?'

'Pity,' Pollard observed, handing back the photograph. 'Did you get anything from the newel staircase?'

'Lovely. There's a nice layer of fine dust on the treads in the middle part, and the prints of those patterned soles of Peplow's shoes were clear as daylight. We took a sample of the dust, and Boyce got a picture. And Peplow's dabs were on the inside and outside handles of the door from the gallery into the passage.'

'Quite simple for him to slip along to the priest's hole while the caretaker was closing up the rooms at the other end of the house. Any trace of a second chap having hidden up?'

'Nix,' replied Toye. 'Not a sign of marks on the carpet under the beds, or hairs or threads caught up underneath. Nor behind the bigger bits of furniture. We even took a look behind the altar frontal in the chapel.'

'All the same, I reckon a chap could've dodged the caretaker easy, and never left a trace, keeping on his feet,' said Strickland, in the tone of a man baulked of his legitimate prey. 'Look at all those rooms upstairs leading out of each other. And tisn't likely the caretaker'd let on if he didn't give the place much of a once-over Tuesday evening.'

'True. Or a chap could have come in after the house was closed, if he'd managed to get hold of keys, or had a pal inside. Grilling Emmett seems to be the next major job, but we must drop in on Lord Seton first, Toye. You boys had better get back to Crockmouth so that Boyce can do his stuff with the photographs. You're busting with curiosity, Boyce. What's biting you?'

'That hair, sir, having seen the lady.'

'The lady,' Pollard said, 'vigorously denied ever having been in the priest's hole, and showed strong distaste at the mere idea.'

He returned to the secretary's office with Toye to find Peggy Blackmore in a state of obvious agitation.

'Lord Seton's engaged for just a few minutes,' she said. 'I'll let him know you're here.'

As she turned to him again Pollard saw that her eyes were full of tears.

'So sorry,' she said, hastily scrubbing with a handkerchief. 'It's just that everything's so ghastly. That wretched man being *killed* by somebody. And now, on top of it all, Whitesisters! I think Maurice Corden's a traitor!'

'Whitesisters? Maurice Corden?' asked Pollard, bewildered.

'He's the consultant we had, and now the Ormistons at Whitesisters have called him in, right on our doorstep, and he's got the nerve to come over here pretending to sympathise. *Whitesisters . . .*'

She broke off hastily as Lord Seton came in, followed by a thin dark man with pronounced features and observant eyes whom he introduced rather cursorily to Pollard as Mr Corden of Stately Homes. The latter proceeded to deplore the increase of country house robberies with overtones of social ease. He became professionally reassuring.

'I've just been warning Lord Seton, Peggy, my dear, that you'll be invaded when Brent reopens. A violent death in historic surroundings is right up the great British Public's street. Now I must dash back to Whitesisters. By the way, and between these four walls, it almost certainly won't be a viable proposition.'

Peggy Blackmore looked unwillingly relieved, and Lord Seton keenly interested.

'I'm not surprised,' he remarked. 'It's an attractive setting, but the house isn't a good specimen of its period, and the whole place has rather run to seed.'

'You're telling me,' replied Maurice Corden. 'It's positively seedy. The Ormistons would have to sink a packet in it to make an opening a commercial proposition, and frankly they haven't got it, and aren't in a position to raise it.'

'Of course they've got some pictures,' Lord Seton said reflectively. 'One or two in the five-figure class at present values, I should think. I only hope they're being kept under proper conditions. Still, if those went, Whitesisters would be even less of a draw. It's really very small, too.'

'That needn't matter, other things being equal. Look at Greenover Manor, for instance . . .'

Pollard listened to this conversation with some surprise. Was it possible that a man personally involved in a violent death in his own house could be so absorbed in business matters?

'I managed to get down on schedule,' Maurice Corden was saying, 'and did my usual local snoop before going over to the Ormistons. I dropped in on the coach people— Blennerhasset's—and the chap in charge there said emphatically that Whitesisters wouldn't be on in the face of your competition here, however much it was tarted up."

Suddenly recalling Pollard's presence, Lord Seton apologetically brought the conversation to an end.

'I must simply fly,' Maurice Corden said, making for the door, 'but I just had to look in. Great to be here again, and I'm utterly convinced that all this brouhaha'll pay off in the end. No, of course I can see myself out . . .'

He vanished.

'Come into the office,' Lord Seton said as the door closed.

Leading the way into the room beyond, he seated himself at his desk, indicating chairs to the others. There were fatigue lines at the corners of his eyes, but Pollard noted with interest that he was far less tense than on the previous night. He told him that investigations in the house itself were now complete and that Brent could be reopened, and he watched him become at once the experienced business man dealing with an unfortunate contretemps.

'Just a word to my secretary, if you don't mind, Superintendent.'

An emotional gasp of relief from Peggy Blackmore was audible over the intercom. Lord Seton pushed a typewritten list across his desk.

'I assumed this would be wanted,' he said, 'and we got it out this morning. A list of everyone on duty on Tuesday afternoon, and in residence here on Tuesday night.'

'Thank you.' Pollard put the list into the case file. 'That'll be a useful time-saver. Last night,' he went on, 'we examined the possibilities of getting out of what I'll call the public wing without leaving a door or window open. I'd like now to discuss the matter of someone being in unauthorised possession of keys, both for getting in and leaving again. With four households here, I expect quite a few people have keys of one kind or another?'

He sensed at once that this question had been expected, and wondered if Lord Seton's categorical rejection of the loophole was deliberate policy. He learnt that when the multiple occupation of Brent was first mooted, all members of the family had been opposed to any idea of communal living. The various households were entirely separate, and none possessed keys to any other. Lord and Lady Seton each had keys to the two doors from their private wing into the public rooms. Mrs Giles Tirle, being responsible for the guides, had a key to the door connecting the first floor of the public wing with her own apartments. Her husband and Lady Arminel Tirle merely had their own front door keys. Emmett was in charge of the keys of the front door, the north gate, and the door from the screens into the courtyard. An emergency set of all keys, including those of the show cases, was kept in the office safe.

A glance showed Pollard that this was of an efficient modern make. He sat for a few moments considering the facts he had just been given. That there was a pointer to Emmett was plain enough. Then he enquired about any incidents of lost or mislaid keys. Lord Seton extracted a key ring from an inner pocket.

'This is my lot,' he said, 'with the car keys and the safe key—there's a duplicate safe key at the bank. At night I put them in a drawer in my dressing room. They've never been missing, and I've never heard of my wife losing hers. Or my brother or sister-in-law for that matter either, and I'm quite sure that I should have heard.'

Pressed about the safe, he insisted that it had never been left unlocked during his absence from the room.

'It's a new safe,' he said, leaning back in his chair with hands thrust into his trouser pockets. 'We put it in when we opened, and some of my wife's jewellery is kept in it, including family pieces. I can fairly say I'm punctilious about it. Another thing I want to say is, Superintendent, that to the best of my knowledge and belief Emmett is a perfectly sound reliable chap. He's been here for ten years.'

'I'm glad to have your opinion of him, and shall keep it in mind,' Pollard replied. 'Just one more question. You've given us a useful list of everyone sleeping on the premises on Tuesday night. Were any regular members of the various households away?'

'Yes. My brother is on a lecture tour in the States. His wife could probably give you his precise whereabouts. His eldest son, an Oxford undergraduate, is in Greece, as far as I know, and his younger boy and my younger daughter are at boarding school. My elder daughter has been with a French family in Paris since Easter, and comes home today.'

'Thank you,' said Pollard, glancing at Toye who was noting down these particulars. 'I don't think we need take up any more of your time at the moment.'

Before they reached the door Peggy Blackmore was being summoned to resume her secretarial duties. Outside in the courtyard Toye turned and raised an interrogative eyebrow.

'Playing it cool, this morning, his lordship, isn't he?' Pollard remarked. 'He doesn't want any truck with my helpful suggestions of somebody having got at keys, or Emmett being involved. Either he knows that he's as safe as houses, or he didn't boot Peplow down those steps. I don't think he can have, you know. It's so hopelessly unconvincing psychologically.'

'Look at him last night,' persisted Toye.

'Might have been suffering from shock. Discovering a stiff in one's home is a bit disconcerting. Or perhaps he thought—wrongly, according to that chap Corden—that all this business would choke off the public. It's all very rum. We'd better go and get something to eat before the inquest at two. It'll be adjourned, of course, and then we'll come back and have a bash at Emmett. I'd like to ring the Yard from a kiosk, and have them just check up on this Giles Tirle in the States. A lecture tour sounds watertight, but you can't be too thorough. One of the newshounds had got on to it, actually. Thanks.'

Pollard stepped through the wicket in the north gate held open for him by Toye, and came face to face with a slim, dark-haired woman in slacks and an open-necked shirt, with a dachshund at her heels. Her resemblance to the originals of many of the family portraits in the hall was beyond question.

'Good morning,' he said. 'May I introduce myself? Detective-Superintendent Pollard of the C.I.D., in charge of the enquiry here. I think I must be speaking to Lady Arminel Tirle?'

'You are.' She gave him a very direct look. 'Do you want to see me? You'll be wasting your time: I'm right off the map here.'

'It's routine, I'm afraid,' Pollard replied. 'We are seeing everyone who was on the premises on Tuesday night. Is it convenient for you to spare a few minutes now, or shall we come back in the later part of the afternoon?'

'As you're here you may as well come in now,' she said briskly, and slipped a latchkey into a lock. Some letters were scattered on the mat, and she stopped to pick them up and glance at them. 'Go straight up, will you, while I just drop this in on the Emmetts: the postman's delivered it here by mistake. My sitting room door's open.'

The sitting room of the flat was at the north-west angle of the house, with views over the gardens and open country beyond. Looking about him Pollard recognised the same combination of business activity and comfortable relaxation as in Lord Seton's office. There was a light quick step on the stairs, and Lady Arminel came in.

'Sit down,' she said without preamble, and took a chair by a window, an alert and upright figure.

'We need only take up a few moments of your time,' Pollard said, realising that a direct conciseness was required. He briefly summarised the known facts about Raymond Peplow and his movements on Tuesday.

'We're anxious to know if he came with a companion.'

'Who hid up, too, and then socked him after a row,' she broke in. 'The obvious explanation, surely?'

'There are other possibilities. Someone getting in with duplicate keys after the house was closed, for instance. Have you ever lost or mislaid your keys, Lady Arminel?'

'Never. Anyway, the only house-key I have is of this flat, and there's no way through.'

'Were you taking parties round on Tuesday afternoon?'

'I don't. Not my line. I run the gardens and the shop.'

'Were you in the shop, then?' persevered Pollard.

'Yes. From two-fifteen to about ten to six. There were a lot of people in on Tuesday.'

'I don't think Raymond Peplow is likely to have patronised the shop,' Pollard said, 'but all the same, I'd like you to look at this photograph of him, and this description of the clothes he was wearing.'

A curious pallor manifested itself under Lady Arminel's sun tan. For a moment she sat absolutely immobile, making no attempt to take the papers held out to her, and then got up abruptly.

'Can't see a thing without my spectacles,' she said.

Pollard watched her searching unconvincingly round the orderly room. Finally she picked up a pair of spectacles from a desk, returned to her chair, put them on and accepted the photograph and typewritten sheet. He saw that her hand was not quite steady at first.

'I'm pretty sure I did see this man,' she said, to his astonishment. 'I didn't notice anyone with him, though.'

Asked about the time when she had seen him, Lady Arminel was definite that it had been towards the end of the afternoon. The garden produce was almost sold out, and she had been regrouping the few remaining punnets of fruit and boxes of cuttings, and chanced to look towards the north gate.

'If it was this Raymond Peplow, he was just standing by himself there, gazing around. He didn't come to buy anything and I didn't see him again.'

Her warm colour and confidence had returned. Puzzled by her reactions Pollard watched her narrowly.

'You didn't recognise him, I suppose, Lady Arminel?'

'No,' she said categorically, 'I didn't. He was a stranger.'

He passed on to Tuesday evening, and learnt that after closing the shop and locking up the day's takings in her flat, she had given the dachshund a run in the grounds. She had then returned home for a bath and leisurely drink, cooked and eaten her supper, and afterwards relaxed over a newspaper. She had rounded off the evening by listening to some records. She had not received any telephone calls.

'Did you hear any disturbance during the evening?'

'Disturbance?'

'Yes. Dogs barking, for instance.'

Pollard watched her make what he was convinced was a genuine effort to recall the evening.

'Now you mention it, there was a bit of a bark-in at one point. The Emmetts' bull terrier, and my brother's hysterical spaniels. I heard it through the music and cursed them. Otto went over to the door and listened, but he's too intelligent to bark just for the hell of it.'

The dachshund's tail thumped the floor enthusiastically at the mention of his name. Pollard dismissed an irrelevant mental picture of an equally engaging animal accompanying a double pram on Wimbledon Common.

'Have you any idea at what time this was?' he asked.

'It wasn't long before I turned in. About half-past ten, I should think.'

Pollard glanced round at Toye, who was completing a note.

'Well, thank you, Lady Arminel,' he said, getting to his feet. 'We needn't keep you any longer. I expect you are in for a busy time, when Lord Seton decides to reopen the house.'

'Lord Seton decides?' she demanded.

'I told him just now that we are through with our investigations on the spot.'

An intent expression came over her face, and he realised that she was hastily reviewing questions of stock and potential sales.

'Please don't bother to come down,' he said. 'We can see ourselves out.'

As they arrived at the car Toye asked if he should drive to the Tirle Arms in Brenting.

'Not on your life,' replied Pollard. 'I'm surfeited with the family as it is. What are they all up to, individually or collectively? Straight back to vulgar Crockmouth for me.'

'Funny how she jibbed at looking at the photo,' Toye remarked as they drove out of the forecourt, 'and then the next minute admitted seeing Peplow, as cool as a cucumber. And putting on an act about her spectacles after reading the address on that letter in a split second.'

'Playing for time, although what for, I can't imagine. Was she expecting to see a photograph of someone else, and if so, who the hell was it?'

At the inquest on Raymond Peplow the Crockmouth coroner, who detested sensationalism, merely took evidence of identity and cause of death, and promptly adjourned the proceedings for three weeks, to the baffled disappointment of those members of the public who had managed to get seats after prolonged queueing. Pollard breathed a sigh of relief, told Strickland and Boyce to get back to the Yard, fobbed off the Press to the best of his ability, and by three o'clock was sitting in the kitchen of the caretaker's house at Brent.

Bill Emmett was a stocky man in his late fifties, whose appearance bore out Lord Seton's testimony of soundness and reliability. He faced Pollard and Toye across the kitchen table, uneasy and sweating slightly, but unshakable under persistent questioning.

'You stick to it that every window and outside door was fastened on the inside when you opened up the public part of the house on Wednesday morning?' Pollard asked.

Emmett passed the tip of his tongue over his lips.

'That's right. Just as I'd left 'em Tuesday evening.'

'Right. I'll buy that. But just when did you leave them all OK on Tuesday evening?'

'Usual time, when I'd done me round. Ten to six, say. Might've bin five to.'

'You told Lady Seton that you'd take a look round with your dog before going to bed on Tuesday night. Did you?'

'What I undertakes, I does,' Emmett replied tersely.

'What time did you do it, and how long were you out?'

He scratched his head, and stared at Pollard with growing hostility.

'Just on ten, I went out. Reckon I was back by quarter past. 'Ere, what's all this in aid of?'

'Did you go alone?'

'I 'ad the dog, same as you said.'

Pollard thrust back his chair, and sat with folded arms, contemplating Emmett.

'Quarter of an hour would be plenty of time for the job, wouldn't it? Just to slip through the front door of the house which you'd left unbolted by arrangement, lock it on the inside and come out by the courtyard door. What did you get for doing it?'

An angry flush mounted on Emmett's face as he assimilated Pollard's remarks.

' 'Ere!' he burst out, 'wot's it you're tryin' to fix on me? It's ruddy lies, start ter finish! I never set foot in the 'ouse from shuttin' up Tuesday to openin' Wednesday mornin'. I'll swear it, and you can't prove no different.'

There was a pause.

'If you've been speaking the truth,' Pollard said deliberately, 'how do you account for the fact that whoever went for Peplow got away without leaving a door or window open?'

' 'Ow the 'ell should I know?' Emmett almost shouted. 'It's your job ter find out, innit? Not mine. Maybe 'e'd got keys. Mrs Giles's place was empty all evenin' up to when she came back with 'is lordship.'

'Could anyone have hidden, and simply walked out after you'd opened the house on Wednesday morning?'

Emmett looked taken aback.

'I 'adn't thought o' that. Could've. Evenin's I takes a good look round, but mornin's I just walks through and opens windows. I'd notice if anythin' was amiss, but I don't go searchin' the place mornin's.'

'Where do you keep the keys of the north gate and the front and courtyard doors?'

'Tryin' to make out as I've left 'em lyin' around, are yer? Upstairs landin' on 'ooks, that's where I keeps 'em. Ask the missis. Ask me daughter.'

'I will.' With a swift movement Pollard got to his feet, took two strides to an inner door, and flung it open before the two startled women on the other side could take evasive action.

'Come in, Mrs Emmett,' he said genially. 'Sorry to have kept you out of your kitchen so long. Is this your daughter?'

She came in, a plump, easy-going woman pink with confusion, and sat down awkwardly on a chair drawn up for her by Toye.

'Yes, that's right,' she said. 'Rosalie, she is.'

The teenage girl who followed her in had been crying, and her green eyeshadow had smudged. At the sight of Pollard and Toye she made an unconvincing would-be provocative movement of her shoulders and slumped on to another chair. Pollard studied her with interest, wondering what aspect of the situation had upset her so much. She was quite pretty, he decided, with a kind of naïve determination in her face.

Mrs Emmett confirmed her husband's statements about

Tuesday evening and the keys in his charge, and Pollard made a show of looking through his notes. He sensed nervous tension on the other side of the kitchen table. Emmett's was understandable enough. His official duties had put him in an invidious position. Mrs Emmett looked faintly aggrieved. Pollard put her down as stupid, comfort-loving, and rather lazy, and resentful of her household's being involved in the unpleasantness of an unexplained death. Rosalie seemed more intelligent than her mother. Was she sharp enough to realise that her father might well come under suspicion, and be frightened by this? But she showed no sign of particular affection for him. . . .

Pollard shut his notebook with a snap which made Mrs Emmett jump. He looked round at the white bull terrier lying couchant in a patch of sunlight, and then back at the Emmetts again.

'What made that dog bark at about half-past ten last Tuesday night?' he rapped out.

Rosalie clapped a hand to her lips. Mrs Emmett's mouth gaped helplessly as she stared at her husband, who promptly went over to the offensive.

'Of all the bloody silly questions you've arst me this past 'alf-hour, that bloody well takes the biscuit,' he shouted. ' 'Oo the 'ell knows wot's goin' on in a dog's 'ead?'

The ensuing silence was broken by a knock at the back door. Bill Emmett leapt to his feet and flung it open. A startled Peggy Blackmore was on the step.

'I'm sorry to disturb you, Superintendent Pollard,' she said, 'but Scotland Yard want you on the telephone.'

Getting up hastily, Pollard thanked her.

'That will be all for the present,' he said to Bill Emmett. 'Good afternoon, Mrs Emmett and Rosalie.'

Within a couple of minutes he was listening to Sergeant Longman in the seclusion of Lord Seton's unoccupied office, noting down the information he had asked for about the inmates of Brent. Lord Seton and his brother had excellent war records and their subsequent civilian careers had been above reproach. The Honourable Giles Tirle could be described as a scholar and pale pink, but had no known political affiliations. He was at present in the States, beyond any doubt. Lady Seton had been hailed in the glossies of her day as the Debutante of the Decade, but had vanished into private life on her marriage. Lady Arminel Tirle had been awarded an M.B.E. for her part in the organisation of the Women's Land Army in the war, and was an active committee member of various bodies concerned with horticulture and the welfare of retired gardeners.

Pollard groaned.

'Haven't you unearthed anything interesting about any of 'em, Longman?' he demanded.

'Hold on a bit, sir. Now the Honourable Mrs Giles Tirle, she's a different cup of tea.'

It appeared that Mrs Giles Tirle, *née* Felicity Openshaw, had a French mother, was bilingual in English and French, and had taken a First in Modern Languages at Oxford. At the beginning of the war she had gone into Intelligence, and a year before D-Day had been parachuted into Occupied France. Narrowly escaping capture by the Nazis on several occasions, she had come through with distinction, and been decorated by both the French and British governments.

'And she's put paid to more than one Hun in her day, I bet,' concluded Sergeant Longman.

'Now this is darned interesting,' said Pollard. 'I'm glad to have it before interviewing the lady. Any more?'

After hearing that nothing was known to the discredit of William Ernest Emmett, Elsie May Emmett, Ada Ellen Pringle or Margaret Blackmore, or of special interest about them, he congratulated Longman on quick results, and rang off. He sat for a moment deep in thought, and then went in search of Toye. They found a garden seat overlooking the rose garden, and he passed on the gist of the information supplied by Longman. Toye listened intently, making careful notes.

'Let's recap,' Pollard said when he came to the end. 'Wash out Nanny Pringle to begin with. She's got the physique of a sparrow. But there's something fishy about all the rest. I don't deny for a moment that Lord Seton was badly het up last night. Granted that it's a bit shattering to find someone's been done in your house, you'd expect more of the stiff upper lip from one of his sort. Then why did the robust Lady Arminel jib at looking at Peplow's photograph? What did she think she was going to see? Can she have a boy friend who's been showing a lot of interest in the miniatures?'

'You wouldn't picture anything of the sort with her,' said Toye seriously.

'No, you wouldn't. Even my imagination won't rise to it, but you never know, of course. As to Lady Seton, her denial of ever having been in the priest's hole was surprisingly energetic, but there are a good many long-haired blondes these days, natural and artificial, aren't there? Coming to the Emmetts, it sticks out a mile that somebody they're anxious to cover turned up at their place at half-past ten on Tuesday night, and we've got to find out who it was. But we won't tackle them again till tomorrow morning.'

'Softening-up effect of a night's worry?'

'Yeah. Toye, what would you expect a woman to be like who'd been in the Resistance?'

Toye considered.

'Cool. Quick-witted. A good liar. Tough as they come.'

'And,' said Pollard thoughtfully, 'quick on the draw and not at all squeamish ... We know Mrs Giles has got a key into the public rooms. Substitute her for Lord Seton in my reconstruction of what might have happened. With the sort of experience she's had, she'd know Peplow was dead. Shutting the panel on him would seem to her the best way out of a tight corner. Maybe that hair's one of hers. Let's go and see if she's a blonde, shall we?'

D

CHAPTER SEVEN

THE Honourable Mrs Giles Tirle was very definitely not a blonde. Tall, with dark hair and eyes, and a strong intelligent face, she came to the front door herself, greeted Pollard and Toye pleasantly and invited them in. She led the way into a large, finely-proportioned room. In spite of some good period furniture it had a comfortable, lived-in air. There were bookcases, a scatter of newspapers and periodicals, a recent much-publicised biography on a chair, and a Siamese cat curled tightly as an ammonite on a windowsill. Photographs of two boys at various stages of growth were dotted about.

'Do, please, sit down,' she said. 'I know you'll be taking notes of the conversation,' she added, turning to Toye with amusement in her voice, 'so there's no need for you to huddle uncomfortably in the background.'

'Forgive me if I begin by telling you a number of facts which you already know, Mrs Tirle,' Pollard said, in response to a politely enquiring glance. He embarked once more on the available information about Raymond Peplow, trying to get her measure as he talked. This is a really formidable personality, he thought.

Felicity Tirle listened to him attentively but without comment. She took the dead man's photograph in a matter-of-fact way, and studied it carefully. Finally she covered first the upper and then the lower part of the face.

'No,' she said at last. 'I'm afraid this doesn't ring a bell at all. There were nearly four hundred visitors on Tuesday, you know, and I naturally concentrated on the parties I took round myself. I'm quite certain this man wasn't

98

among them. May I see the description of the clothes you mentioned?'

As she read it, Pollard watched interest appear in her face.

'Now, this does remind me of something,' she told him. 'I'm half French, and often go over to see my mother's people. Until this moment I've never thought about it, but I suppose I accept the different cut of men's clothes on the Continent as a fact of life. I distinctly remember looking out of the Library window when I was with my last party of the day, and noticing in a casual way that there was a foreign male in my sister-in-law's lot in the forecourt.'

'Did you notice his face?' Pollard asked, with a growing sense of wariness.

'No, unfortunately. It was simply that his clothes happened to catch my eye. I can only remember that he had dark hair.'

'Did you see him at any time later in the afternoon?'

'No. I'm quite sure about that. When I brought my party down the main staircase at the end of their tour, I saw that there was a bit of a mix-up between the two next lots, my sister-in-law's being one of them. I took a good look at them in case I felt I ought to weigh in and lend a hand, and I certainly didn't notice the man again then.'

'Did you, in fact, weigh in, Mrs Tirle?'

'No,' she replied easily. 'I decided that the two guides would be able to cope. There was no one following on: we don't admit to the house after five. I came back here, and thankfully made myself a cup of tea.'

Her eyes were on his face, with an expression of faint amusement.

Pollard switched abruptly to another topic.

'I suppose that when you joined Lord and Lady Seton to go over to Fulminster, you would cut through the public rooms to reach their wing?'

'Good heavens, no!' Felicity Tirle exclaimed with mock horror. 'We all feel most strongly about the self-contained aspect of our homes. Have quite a thing about it, in fact. I went down and round, if you follow me. In any case, I don't possess a key to the door from the public rooms into the west wing.'

'I see,' said Pollard. 'And when you returned shortly before midnight, you came in by way of your own front door? I'm sure you see the point of all these questions, Mrs Tirle?'

'Certainly I do. It sticks out a mile. To answer the last one, my brother-in-law dropped me outside my front door before driving round to his own, as he will have already told you, no doubt.'

Pollard had an exasperating feeling of being deftly out-manoeuvred.

'Was this flat empty while you were at Fulminster?' he asked rather abruptly.

'To the best of my knowledge and belief, yes. I only have daily domestic help, and my husband and two sons are away.'

'Has anyone contacted you to say they rang you at about nine-forty on Tuesday evening, and couldn't get an answer?'

'No one.'

For the first time he felt that he had taken her by surprise.

'I want you,' he said, 'to think back to last Tuesday night, after you came home from Fulminster. Can you remember anything, however trivial, which struck you as unusual?'

Felicity Tirle frowned slightly, and seemed to hesitate.

'It really is hardly worth mentioning, especially as I may quite well have imagined it. I was tired when I got in, and went straight to bed. I read for about ten minutes, and then put my light out and went to sleep almost at once. The next thing I knew was that I was sitting bolt upright in bed, convinced that a door had slammed. It was daylight —ten minutes past five. I listened, but everything was perfectly quiet, and I decided that I had had one of my tiresome recurring nightmares. You may know something about my war service.'

'I do,' Pollard replied, 'and greatly respect you for it, if I may say so. But I rather think that you did get up, Mrs Tirle, and went to see that all was well in the public rooms.'

'You're quite mistaken,' she replied urbanely. 'I lay down and went to sleep again, only too glad that it wasn't time to get up. You know, I don't quite see the point of this suggestion, unless'—she looked at him quizzically—'you suspect me of carrying over the least mentionable of my Resistance activities into civilian life.'

'I wonder who trained her for Occupied France?', Pollard said, as he and Toye were making for the car a few minutes later. 'You spotted the technique, of course? However good and convincing a liar you are, nothing but the actual truth ever has quite the authentic ring, as we well know. So you include some verifiable facts in your statements, which makes it a lot easier to get deliberately misleading stuff across. I'm positive she's either involved in this affair herself, or knows something about it.'

'Could she have been in with Peplow on the theft idea, seeing she's half a foreigner herself? International racket of some sort?' propounded Toye.

'In theory, yes. But after all, she's the heir's mother. Would she go in for looting the family treasures?'

'Insurance?'

'You might have got something there. None of them seem to be hard up, but we could have their finances vetted more thoroughly. The thing that interests me is the slamming door yarn. I've got a hunch that's one of the true bits. Was it Peplow's basher making off? But Dr Netley, you remember, put the latest possible time of death at five on Wednesday morning, and he'll have safeguarded himself by allowing a margin. So why should the chap have hung around like that, for heaven's sake? It's broad daylight by that hour at this time of year. Once again, it doesn't make sense.'

'I reckon you're dead right about the lady getting up and going through to the public rooms,' Toye said, settling himself at the wheel and letting in the clutch. 'She wouldn't turn a hair at the thought of meeting a burglar, not after the Gestapo. Mostly likely she's still got a gun, and took it along. Suppose she found that panel open, and looked down and saw the body. Women've got a funny way of looking at things. She might have thought it would make less of an upset for the family if it wasn't found till a lot of visitors were in the place.'

'Too intelligent, and too much know-how, I think, like Lord Seton. If she was mixed up with Peplow, of course . . . Wait a bit, though. Did she go in, and find a door open, and decide to shut it? That would explain how someone got away without trace, and it lets Emmett out.'

'That's more like it,' exclaimed Toye. 'Proves she was involved though, doesn't it? If not, and she thought there'd been a break-in, why didn't she raise the alarm?'

There was a stream of traffic on the main road, and he drew up at the gates.

'There are possible explanations of that,' Pollard said thoughtfully. 'She might have checked up, and found nothing was disturbed or missing, and come to the conclusion that Emmett had overlooked the door, and that she'd heard it just banging in the wind. Or, of course, if she *was* involved, the whole thing might have been pre-arranged. But that still leaves us with the difficulty of the time. People get up early in the country, even these days.'

The car shot out in a brief lull, and headed for Crockmouth.

'Going back to Emmett, there's those dogs creating ten-thirty Tuesday night,' Toye reminded him.

'Blast the dogs, and everyone else in the ruddy place,' Pollard retorted with feeling. 'Look here, we simply must get what facts we've got down on paper, and see if they add up to anything. I doubt it. The whole business is haywire. We'll make them lay on a cuppa at the station, and then have a go.'

On arrival they were greeted with a request to look in on Superintendent Perry, a tall, gaunt man with small sagacious eyes which reminded Pollard of an elephant's. He was a firm believer in delegating responsibility, and hastened to explain that Inspector Diplock had had to go out on a job.

'One more break-in. A packet of valuable stuff lifted, too. You think people might have learnt to take a few simple precautions after all the propaganda we've put out, wouldn't you? I told Diplock I'd pass on a couple of reports that have come in for you. Put the tray down there,' he ordered a constable who had appeared with tea. 'Pour it out yourselves, the way you like it.'

'Thanks,' replied Pollard, helping himself, and pushing the tray over to Toye. 'Got anything useful for us? We can do with it.'

'Dr Netley's report, to start with. It's full of possible alternatives and qualifying statements, but the gist is that there's no trace of poison or dope. Peplow'd only taken a dollop of whisky and a small quantity of food within about six hours of his death.'

'Any narrowing down of the probable time of death?'

Superintendent Perry grinned.

'You won't catch Dr Netley risking a challenge in court from another medico. All he says is that in his personal opinion death is more likely to have taken place before midnight than after. But if you want my comment on that, you can bet he's right. He's a very sound chap on his own line. Any help to you?'

'It could be, I suppose. At the moment we've got on to a rather fishy phone call to Brent at nine-forty on Tuesday evening, and a suggestion that somebody may have scarpered from the public part at ten past five on Wednesday morning.'

'Your headache, not mine, thanks be. The next thing is that we've found out where Peplow lunched on Tuesday for you.'

Pollard was warm in his congratulations.

'Tell your C.C. he can call us in any time he likes,' he said.

'He picked the Magnificent,' Superintendent Perry continued, concealing obvious gratification. 'It's a big new place, very posh and pricey. Packed at this time of year. Wonderful where the money comes from, isn't it?'

Pollard agreed that it was.

'How do the times work out?' he asked.

'Reasonably. Unless Peplow came down on the 1.50 a.m. which I should think we can rule out, he'd've got the 9.30 from Paddington, getting in here at 11.45. Our chaps have been on to the taxi rank, but none of the boys seem to have driven him anywhere. If he'd walked to the pub, he'd've had ample time to drop in at Blennerhasset's and book a seat. There's a barman at the Magnificent who's pretty sure he served him sometime round a quarter to one, and one of the waiters took a look at the photo and the description of the clothes, and said he'd swear to him. He seems to have been in the dining room from about one to two, lunching alone. After that nobody seems to have noticed him around until he joined the coach about ten to three.'

'How could he have known there would be a coach trip to Brent? Doesn't it point to his having been down last week for a recce?'

'Needn't. Blennerhasset advertises his trips in that guide to Brent that Peplow had on him. Gives the times and everything. The daily trip they run in the season goes at two-fifteen, but if there's a demand, they put on a later one as well, usually going along the coast first, and having tea at a joint called the Wreckers before turning up at Brent. Peplow was in luck on Tuesday. The later trip being on meant that he didn't have to hang about so long at Brent. By the way, the C.C.'s been in, asking about a conference on the case.'

Pollard groaned.

'Try to head him off a bit longer, there's a good chap. There's damn little to confer about up to now.'

'OK,' promised Superintendent Perry. 'I'll do my best. I'm not hard up for jobs myself, come to that.'

'Thanks. We'll push off and leave you to get on with it.'

The room allotted to the Yard team was small and stuffy. Pollard flung up the window, and gazed across the car park at the depressing backs of a row of houses. He was seized with one of his periodic spasms of loathing for his job, and the squalid conditions under which so much of it had to be done. At this time of day most chaps were making for their homes and gardens... The sound of Toye moving chairs with unnecessary vigour brought him sharply back to reality. Peeling off his coat he draped it over the window-sill, and sat down at the inconveniently small table.

'Let's draw up a timetable first,' he said. 'It clears the mind a bit.'

According to their usual practice they first worked independently, then compared the results, and finally produced a fair copy of a finished version.

Tuesday, 10 July (approximate times)

a.m.

11.45   Peplow arrives at Crockmouth railway station

p.m.

12.45   Peplow in bar of Magnificent (?)
1.00   Peplow lunching in the hotel until 2.00 p.m.
3.15   Peplow joins coach trip
4.45   Coach arrives at Brent
5.00   Peplow gives Cudwinkle message for driver
5.30   House closed to public. Emmett starts locking up
5.50   Emmett finishes his round. Lady Arminel closes shop
6.00   Grounds of Brent closed to public
6.30   Lord Seton returns from London

7.00	Lord and Lady Seton and Mrs Giles Tirle leave for Fulminster
9.40	Mrs Pringle gets wrong number call, and at once hears the Giles Tirles' telephone ringing
10.00	Emmett goes out with dog for look round
10.15	Emmett returns to his quarters
10.30	Emmett's dog and the Seton spaniels bark
10.50	Lady Arminel goes to bed
11.00	Mrs Pringle goes to bed. Seton spaniels on front door mat

Wednesday, 11 July

a.m.

12.20	Lord Seton in bed. Lady Seton in bath
12.50	Lady Seton wakes up in her bath, sees that it is nearly 1.00 a.m., and hurries to bed, finding her husband asleep
5.10	Mrs Giles Tirle hears door slam

p.m.

| 12.15 | Mrs Lessinger discovers Peplow's body in priest's hole |

Toye carefully screwed on the cap of his pen, and replaced the latter in his pocket. Pollard pushed back his chair, and sat with his legs stretched out in front of him, contemplating the timetable through the smoke of his cigarette.

'The thing that sticks out,' he remarked presently, 'is that Lord Seton had roughly half an hour, and Mrs Tirle the whole blessed night in which they could have done the job. On paper Emmett's even better placed, with a possible earlier start. As far as the others go, well, at times you've got to use commonsense in default of actual evidence. I'm prepared to rule out Lady Seton and Mrs Pringle provisionally, and Lady Arminel for the moment, although I expect she could have managed to get herself keys if she'd wanted to.'

'If Dr Netley's right about death having occurred before

midnight, doesn't it point to Emmett?' Toye suggested.

'Yes, it does. But as principal or accessory, do you think? Somehow I can't see him as the actual killer, you know. He's a simple blustering soul, without any subtlety or poise to him. Could he have faced Lord Seton, and Diplock, and the rest of us without giving himself away, if he'd accidentally killed Peplow? I very much doubt it. He could so easily maintain that he was defending his employer's property... expect a lot of kudos, in fact, for tackling a burglar. But if he was merely an accessory, we're up against X again. I'm getting X in my hair. He just won't tie up with Peplow sitting for hours in that stinking hole, all fitted out to bust open the showcases and escape with the loot.'

There was a lengthy silence, finally broken by Toye.

'Next thing's another go at the Emmetts, I take it, sir?'

'We'll go over first thing tomorrow morning. It shouldn't be too difficult to break them down about their caller that night, with the three of them in it. Hell—who's this? Come in!'

A solemn-faced young constable entered, saluting smartly.

'Lady asking to see you, sir. A Mrs Flack, from London. She says she's deceased's sister.'

'Good lord!' exclaimed Pollard. 'Well, I suppose it's not all that surprising. She could have seen one of the midday editions, or heard something on the one o'clock news.'

'That's right, sir. That's what she says—the one o'clock news.'

'Hasn't she been in touch with her local station or the Yard?'

'I don't think so, sir. She said she'd come down here by the next train.'

'What's she like?'

The constable anxiously searched his vocabulary to find an appropriate word.

'Very respectable, sir,' he pronounced at last.

'Bring her along, will you?' said Pollard, snatching up

his coat. 'And we'll have to fit in another chair.'

Mrs Flack had a pale lifeless face, and wore the muted out-of-date clothes of a middle-aged woman of her type in modestly comfortable circumstances. As he shook her limp hand Pollard scrutinised her face, and fancied he could detect a faint resemblance to Raymond Peplow.

'Do sit down, Mrs Flack,' he said. 'It's very helpful of you to come along so promptly.'

She subsided on to the chair proffered by Toye, sitting upright and clutching a large black handbag on her lap.

'I felt it was only right to come,' she said in a flat voice with a cockney edge. 'My hubby, he thought the same. He comes home to his lunch, and we always turn on the news, one o'clock. He'd've come with me, only for them being short-handed at the shop with the holidays. I'm Ray's sister, and there's no other relatives near enough to matter. But I'm not certain I'll know him for sure, not after all this time. 1935 it was, when he went off.'

'You mean he left home in 1935?' Pollard asked.

'That's right. Without as much as a word to any of us. Mum and Dad never properly got over it.'

'Didn't you hear from him again?'

'Only the post card next morning, saying he was sick of Finchley, and was going to see a bit of the world. Last we ever heard of him, that was.'

'I suppose your parents contacted the police? How old was your brother?'

'Just short of eighteen. No, Dad wasn't going to bring the police into it. He was sure Ray'd got into trouble, and that was why he made off. No end of a worry he'd been ever since he left school. Never held down a job for more than a month or two. Then he'd got in with a nasty lot of Reds, and went to their meetings. It made Dad real wild.'

'He's not in our records in this country, Mrs Flack,' Pollard told her. 'Nor in those of the police in the Argentine as far as anything criminal goes. As you probably heard on the news, he's been living out there since 1937.'

'You'd think he might have given a thought to his own flesh and blood, not to mention coming back to fight for his country, instead of skulking in a foreign country while the bombs were coming down on London.'

Mrs Flack gave an indignant sniff.

Feeling some sympathy for Raymond Peplow, Pollard turned to the matter in hand.

'We don't want to distress you, Mrs Flack, but I'm sure you understand that it's very important for us to get a positive identification of your brother. Will you think back to the time before he left home, and try to picture him in your mind? Take your time. Try to remember your family life in those days...Now, had Ray any distinguishing marks of any kind? Birthmarks, for instance, or operation scars?'

Mrs Flack stared straight in front of her with lack-lustre eyes.

'There's nothing of that sort I can call to mind,' she said at last. 'It's so long ago, and a lot's happened since then, what with the war, and one thing and another. Mum and Dad's gone, of course. Dark, Ray was. Not out of the ordinary tall or short. There were photos, but they went in the blitz, else I'd've brought them...'

Her voice trailed off. Pollard waited patiently. He was on the point of broaching the subject of a visit to the mortuary when she suddenly spoke again.

'Why, I'd forgotten about his teeth. Dreadful teeth he had, right from a child. He had to have a top plate by the time he left school.'

The silence which followed was so prolonged that she looked up to find Pollard's eyes riveted on her.

'Mrs Flack,' he said, 'the man who was killed at Brent isn't your brother, then.'

Leaving Toye to get the bewildered Mrs Flack's signature to her statement, and give her any necessary assistance for her return journey to London, Pollard went to put through a call to the Yard which took some time. Its upshot was the setting on foot of some fresh enquiries, including one on Mrs Flack herself, and arrangements for submitting Raymond Peplow's photograph to the authorities in Argentina for identification at the earliest possible moment. He found the room empty on his return, and rightly surmised that Toye had driven Mrs Flack to the railway station. He picked up her signed statement from the table, and was reading it when Toye came in.

'She got her train all right,' he told Pollard. 'Where do we go from here, sir?'

Pollard threw down Mrs Flack's statement.

'Ahead as planned, until it's known if the chap in the mortuary is the chap who's been calling himself Raymond Peplow for the past thirty years. If he is, I can't see that his real identity can concern us much after all this time, can you? If he isn't, there'll have to be an all-out drive to identify him, and track down the Argentine Peplow, assuming he's still above ground.'

Toye looked gloomy.

'It only wanted this, didn't it? As if it wasn't snarled up enough already.'

'Either way,' Pollard said, 'our job's to find out who did the chap we've got. And it seems to me we can't do much more about it tonight. Going back to where we were when Mrs Flack blew in, we've sorted things out a bit, and it's perfectly clear who are at the top of the list where opportunity goes. And means, too. Putting in the boot isn't a usual female technique, but Mrs Tirle's not a usual sort of woman. She's well-built, into the bargain. Motive? There's no need to look for one in the ordinary sense. I'm convinced it was a case of going for a burglar a bit too hard, probably in self-defence. The man was armed, I expect.'

'Wonder what happened to the gun?' said Toye.

'Brent's the hell of a big place, isn't it? Let's call it a day, shall we? Go and eat, or what?'

A few minutes later they parted company, Toye heading

for a quick snack and a cinema, his favourite means of mental relaxation on a case. Pollard had a more leisurely meal, rang Jane at extravagant length, and, feeling more cheerful, strolled along the sea front before turning in. He noticed that a lot of people seemed to be wandering about and sitting around with an air of expectation, and idly wondered why. Suddenly a fireworks display leapt into being from the region of the pier. He perched on the sea wall, and watched the brilliantly coloured patterns explode into being against the darkening sky, hang poised and interlaced, and abruptly vanish. Their intricacy suggested his problem. The parallel had hardly struck him when a loud bang heralded a vivid streak of red fire, which ripped across a display of golden fountains, seeming to obliterate it.

People near him laughed.

'Somebody pressed the wrong button,' a man remarked.

Nice if it could work out that way, Pollard thought ... He yawned hugely, realised that he was short of sleep, and set off for his hotel.

CHAPTER EIGHT

POLLARD seldom planned in advance the line he would take when interviewing suspects. On the following morning he reacted at once to Bill Emmett's attempt to keep Rosalie out of the enquiry by resolving to concentrate on her.

'You were all in this house on Tuesday night, and I must see you all,' he said. 'Rosalie is under age, and I prefer to question her with her parents present. Where is she?'

Bill Emmett, looking truculent with his shirtsleeves rolled up, muttered something about the tea room and made for the door, where he was neatly intercepted by Toye.

'Sergeant, go over to the tea room, and ask Rosalie to come and see me at her home,' Pollard said.

The kitchen was stuffy, smelling of fried breakfast and detergent. There was a tense wait on hard chairs drawn up to the table. At last footsteps were heard, and Rosalie came in, escorted by Toye. Her eyes went straight to her father, not to her rather sulky-looking mother.

'Come an' sit b' yer Dad, luv,' he said, pulling a chair closer.

Utterly spoilt by a doting father and a mum too lazy to stand up to her, Pollard thought. What's she been up to, I wonder?

'Rosalie,' he said, suddenly getting his cue, 'when I saw you so unhappy yesterday afternoon I knew you were the person who could help me about last Tuesday night.' He watched her eyes widen with apprehension as he talked. 'When a pretty girl like you gets upset, it's always the same reason, isn't it? Just the boy-friend.'

For a second the whole family stared at him dumbfounded.

Then Rosalie's lower lip quivered, and without warning she burst into the loud boo-hoos of a small child, punctuated by disjointed words.

'...no difference to no one...only jus' sleepin' here ...gone jus' after five nex' mornin'...got in on time...'

Checking an attempt by Bill Emmett to intervene, Pollard spoke to her sharply.

'Stop this ridiculous noise, Rosalie, and be your age,' he ordered. 'Who slept here on Tuesday night?'

'M-y boy friend. Dick White,' she hiccupped.

Eventually the whole story came out. Dick White was a van driver for Crunchaway Limited, a Midland firm manufacturing savoury crisps and snacks. He was the step-son of Mrs Emmett's sister, and lived in Warhampton. The two families were on friendly terms, and Dick and Rosalie had become engaged some months earlier. Her father, however, had refused to give his consent to the marriage until Rosalie was eighteen. Normally Dick was on Crunchaway's Lancashire run, but had jumped at the chance of running an extra consignment down to Crockmouth on one of his days off.

Crunchaway's rule was that any of their vans arriving too late for delivery that day should be parked overnight in an official enclosure for commercial vehicles. Dick White had been quick to see the possibility of a bogus breakdown, and a night at the Emmetts'. By making an early start the next morning he could ensure being on time for his first delivery. Bill Emmett had opposed the plan at first, but as usual, Rosalie had had her way. Dick had parked his van in a disused sandpit on the Brent estate, and arrived at the caretaker's house just after ten-thirty on Tuesday night, the sound of his footsteps alerting Snowball, who had barked.

Pollard listened with a growing conviction that he was hearing the truth, and the possibility of the Emmetts' visitor being connected with the events in the miniatures room receded rapidly in his mind. He asked a number of questions, but the account of Dick White's arrival never varied. The young man had cut across the park on foot. Under cover of Snowball's barking Rosalie had slipped out and let him in by the wicket in the north gate. They had all sat down to a bit of hot supper, and afterwards the parents had tactfully gone up to bed, leaving the young couple in the kitchen. Bill Emmett, however, did not hold with goings-on before marriage, and had warned Rosalie that if the pair of them weren't up by twelve, he'd be down to fetch her in his nightshirt. He had stayed awake long enough to see that his orders were carried out, and heard the pair going to their respective rooms. Dick's, immediately above Mr and Mrs Emmetts', had floorboards which gave earsplitting creaks at every step. After inspecting it, Pollard was convinced that he could not have left the house and returned to it undetected during the night.

On the landing he paused in front of a bunch of keys hanging on a nail.

'Do you leave these here overnight?' he asked.

'I takes 'em into the bedroom,' Bill Emmett replied heatedly. 'An' if you think me wife's sister's husband's lad—'

'I'm paid to think,' Pollard cut in shortly. 'I'm carrying out a routine enquiry which could have been over and done with yesterday afternoon, if you had behaved like a sensible man.'

He continued downstairs, where Rosalie and her mother were sitting in a deflated silence.

'I shall have to interview Dick White, to see if he can confirm what you have all told me,' he said. 'May I have his address, please?'

At this Rosalie showed signs of bursting into tears again.

'He'll get the sack if his boss hears of it,' she quavered.

'If he can give a satisfactory account of himself, his boss may not have to come into it,' he told her.

'Oh, thank you,' she gasped, pink with relief as she wrote the address on the back of an envelope.

'Blame meself,' remarked Bill Emmett gloomily.

Pollard glanced at him.

'Neither,' he said, 'are we interested in unauthorised parking on Lord Seton's property.'

It struck him that the relief exhibited by the Emmett family over side issues was convincing evidence of their lack of complicity in the graver one.

'Sergeant Toye will now write out a summary of what you have told us,' he said. 'Then he'll read it to you. If you agree that it's a fair record, he'll ask you to sign it. I'll be around, sergeant, when you're through.'

Leaving the house he went out of the north gate, and past the tea room to the seat which he had occupied with Toye on the previous afternoon. He felt depressed. In his own mind he was certain that Dick White and the Emmetts were in the clear. Back again to Lord Seton, Mrs Giles, and Persons Unknown, in inexplicable possession of keys or incredible cahoots with other members of the household.

It was a glorious July morning. The fragrance of hundreds of roses came drifting to him on a light breeze. Away to his left the great house dreamed in the sunlight, but its dominating quality was in evidence all the same. Pollard closed his eyes resolutely, and began to shape the report he would make to the Assistant Commissioner that evening.

Suddenly conscious of being no longer alone, he opened them again. A small gnomelike figure with wispy white hair was contemplating him with undisguised interest.

'Yew be one o' they Lunnon 'tecs?' the little old man asked. 'One o' they perlice chaps as us sees on the telly? I likes they perlice programmes.'

'Do you?' replied Pollard. 'Yes, I'm from the Yard. You work here, I expect?'

'Aye. Sam Webber's the name. Man an' boy I've worked yur, savin' the fust war. Too old fer 'Itler's, I wur. Fust under 'is present lordship's granfer, then under 'is pa, and now 'im, Roger, eighth Earl o' Seton. That's 'im. Now us be open to public, I be car park attendant afternoons. Mornin's I clears up an' clips the 'edges over to the maze.

'Ave 'ee 'ad a go, zur? Maybe yew'd find summat worthwhile in the middle of 'n.'

Sam Webber indicated trim box hedges to the right of the rosegarden, and gave Pollard so knowing a look that he was intrigued in spite of himself. He glanced at his watch, and jingled the loose change in his pocket.

'What's the drill?' he asked. 'I can only spare a few minutes.'

Sam Webber gave an unmistakably lewd cackle.

'Fust right, fust left till 'ee gets there, zur, an' t'other way comin' out.'

Pollard passed over a tip.

'Misleading the police is an offence,' he remarked, evoking another cackle.

As he reached the entrance to the maze he looked back, and saw the old man positively hugging himself. Uninhibited classical statuary? He had taken a couple of right turns when he suddenly knew for a certainty that his arrival was being uneasily awaited.

Another couple of seconds brought him out into a gravelled space in which there were two rustic seats. On one of them, at an exaggerated distance apart, sat a young man with the distinctive Tirle features and a very pretty girl. The young man, wearing light trousers, a check shirt and rope sandals, rose politely to his feet.

'Good morning, sir,' he said. 'It's Detective-Superintendent Pollard of the Yard, isn't it? I hope we haven't obliterated any clues?'

Pollard returned the greeting, including them both.

'To be honest,' he said, 'at this moment I'm merely wasting the taxpayer's money. Mazes intrigue me. You must be Mrs Giles Tirle's eldest son, I think, and you,' he smiled at the girl, 'Lady Caroline Tirle.'

'Caroline Tirle,' she replied, giving him an engaging grin. 'Except when I'm blatantly cashing in on the handle. *Liberté, égalité, fraternité*, in these days, you know.'

'Don't mind my cousin,' Robert Tirle remarked with

excessive detachment, 'She's just back from some unfortunate family in France. Something had to be done about her accent.'

'Hybrid and intellectual snob,' returned Caroline Tirle, sedulously avoiding his eye. 'Couldn't you sit down and talk to us just for a minute, Mr Pollard? I've never met anyone from the Yard before. This affair's a terrific thrill. We can't help, worse luck: we were both away till last night. I'm dying to ask you all sorts of things.'

'The most abysmal nit who goops in front of a TV screen would know the police don't answer questions, I should have thought.'

Robert addressed the remark to Pollard, who sat down, once more intrigued. Why, they're in love, he thought.

'Tell me what it feels like to have your home open to the public,' he said.

'With it,' Caroline replied promptly. 'There's hardly a Stately Home left with its gates closed. It's practically that or National Assistance, you know. But it's a bore, let's face it. Bang goes the summer.'

'It's better than living on a shoestring under a leaking roof,' Robert commented. 'Or opting out. I'm trad at heart, I suppose.'

'He's the heir,' Caroline told Pollard. 'There's only me and a sister. Mummy had to have a hysterectomy,' she added explicitly.

It struck him that the pair were interesting blends of the older generation. Robert Tirle was a more subtle edition of his aunt, Lady Arminel, and had inherited his mother's intelligence. Caroline had a more robust version of her mother's beauty, and, he suspected, something of her father's acumen and drive. Enquiries had revealed that Robert was reading Greats on a New College scholarship, and had just completed his third year. Asked about his future, he admitted to the possibility of a First. If it came off, it would probably be the Foreign Office or the Diplomatic.

'Then when I've had all the red tape and protocol I

can take,' he said, 'I'll opt out, and come back and put Brent across in the current idiom.'

'I've flatly refused to try for a university,' Caroline announced. 'I'm an intelligent unacademic. It's a terribly important section of the community: it practically runs the country, actually. I shall be a Third or Fourth Girl in a London flat when I go to a secretarial college in September, if I can wear down the parents. They think I'm going to live with a suffocatingly square sister of Mummy's.'

'Lady Caroline,' said Pollard, 'when were you last down in the priest's hole?'

They both looked at him quickly, and he watched her colour slightly and dart a glance at her cousin.

'Wasn't it in the Christmas vac?' Robert came in with studied casualness. 'That wet day we went down for a giggle.'

Pollard's expression remained politely interrogative.

'It may sound a shade off-beat,' Caroline said with a touch of hauteur. 'In fact, the idea wasn't what a bloody-minded person would think.'

'It certainly wasn't.' Robert spoke with decision. 'And frankly, I don't see its relevance to what you're down here for.'

'I don't think I'm bloody-minded,' Pollard said tranquilly. 'Just trying to tie up loose ends, like a conscientious policeman. We found a long golden hair caught on the stonework of the priest's hole. Lady Seton assured us that she had never been inside it, so when I saw that Lady Caroline had hair of the same type, I thought I would check up.'

'Sorry if I was snooty,' Caroline told him. 'It's a sore subject. Don't look all disapproving, Robert. It's OK to talk to the police as long as you're not a criminal. It's like the confessional for RCs. You see, Mr Pollard, we got engaged at Christmas, and when we told the family they hit the roof. There was such a stink that we suddenly felt we'd got to get away from it all. It was pouring with rain, so I thought of the hole.'

'Misguided melodrama,' said Robert, showing slight discomfort. 'It was so foul down there that we crawled out after about five minutes, laughing ourselves sick. Cold, dank and murder to the bottom. It hadn't occurred to us to take cushions to sit on. The engagement stands, by the way. As soon as we're both of age we shall announce it—unless the parents give in before then.'

'I expect they feel you're both a bit young for a formal engagement.'

'It's only partly that,' Caroline told Pollard. 'They're still harping on the first cousin business, although everyone knows that was exploded long ago. But what's really behind it is Family, in block capitals. There's an Undesirable Streak in the Tirles, you know. They see a generation of drop-outs and meths drinkers ahead, and the old ancestral home full of squatters. Robert's young brother's got it. He's already been expelled from three schools. Our young would have it on both sides, you see.'

'Paul's equalled Uncle Oliver's record already,' added Robert. 'Of course Uncle O. was sent down from Oxford, too, but Paul won't even get there in these democratic days.'

'Where is your Uncle Oliver now?' asked Pollard with some amusement.

'His mortal remains are forming the corner of a foreign field that is for ever England. I wouldn't care to speculate further. He stopped a bomb while fighting for the Left in the Spanish Civil War. We don't mention him. His memorial tablet in Brenting church is the epitome of reticence.'

Pollard realised that he was holding his breath. There was a sudden and almost audible click in his mind.

'Was your uncle your father's elder brother?' he asked Caroline.

'His elder half-brother, to be exact. My grandfather married twice. Aunt Arminel and Uncle Oliver were the first family. Think what he let us in for! Not that I don't adore it all at times,' she admitted frankly.

Pollard glanced at his watch and stood up. Robert Tirle courteously followed suit.

'I'm afraid I must be off: my sergeant will be wondering where I've got to. It's been nice of you both to tell me about yourselves. May I wish you luck, however things turn out?'

They murmured rather inarticulate thanks. He knew with sudden conviction that this pair, so lavishly endowed by nature and circumstance, would not only marry, but make a go of it.

'Would you like an escort, sir?' Robert asked. 'Or do you somehow know the drill? You came in like a homing pigeon.'

'I go into reverse, I take it? First left, first right.'

'I know,' said Caroline. 'Sam Webber, the old traitor. Be seeing you, I hope, Mr Pollard.'

He arrived at the car somewhat breathless. Toye, already established at the wheel, looked at him in surprise.

'The church,' Pollard said, getting in hastily. 'Down in the village somewhere. I'll explain—or try to—as we go.'

As he talked, he had the gratification of hearing a startled Toye crash his gears, swear briefly and apologise.

'Cor lumme,' he added, and lapsed into a staggered silence as they drew up outside the church.

Preoccupied though he was, Pollard noted the latter's architectural merits. There was a fine Norman west door, and sturdy Norman pillars at the western end of the nave. The chancel had been lengthened later, and had three beautiful Early English lancet windows... Pity the place was so crowded with monuments to departed Tirles, interesting though some of them were.

His reflections were interrupted by an exclamation from Toye, who pointed to a vigorous and unusually well-preserved fresco of the Last Judgement. As usual, the aghast horror of the damned, struggling out of their coffins to find themselves awaited by gloating devils armed with pitchforks, made the stiff angelic reception of the emergent blessed look tame.

'Enough to give you the willies,' commented Toye.

'Come on,' said Pollard. 'We're looking for a memorial tablet to Oliver Tirle, eldest son of the seventh earl. It'll be small and somewhere inconspicuous, I fancy.'

In the end he found it himself, tucked away in the north aisle, and obscured by a monstrous eulogistic monument to the second Lady Seton, who had died in childbirth in the late eighteenth century. Its wording could hardly have been more concise.

OLIVER MARCHMONT TIRLE, VISCOUNT LAMBROOKE
1917-1937
Killed in an air raid
in Spain

1937, he thought, staring at it. And in the autumn of 1937, the chap calling himself Raymond Peplow turned up in the Argentine. My God, what have I unearthed this time? Turning to summon Toye, his eye was caught by the spectacle of the dead rising from their graves.

'Ironic,' he said aloud. 'Death on Doomsday.'

'The Old Man,' Pollard said to Jane at a late hour that night, in the tone of one reporting an historic event, 'sat bolt upright...'

'Evening, Pollard,' the Assistant Commissioner had remarked from his usual semi-recumbent position behind his desk. 'So your chap in the priest's hole isn't this Raymond Peplow after all, I gather?'

'No, sir,' Pollard replied. 'Confirmation's come through that he was the chap from the Argentine who's been calling himself Raymond Peplow for the past thirty years all right, but actually I think he was the lawful eighth Earl of Seton.'

At this point the historic event previously mentioned took place. Pollard saw an expression of pure glee come into the A.C.'s face. A lift of an eyebrow instructed him to proceed. He took a deep breath and plunged.

'So you see, sir,' he concluded, 'I think there must have been a chance resemblance between Viscount Lambrooke and Peplow, and that they both landed up in the British contingent of the International Brigade in the Spanish Civil War. From what his sister said, Peplow may have been a convinced Communist. According to the young Tirles, there's a latent wild streak in the family, and it came out in Lambrooke, who was a natural rebel. He had been expelled from various schools and sent down from Oxford, and might have joined the International Brigade just for the hell of it. As it happens, I read a book on the Civil War not long ago. A good many of the Brigade were completely disillusioned by the spring of 1937, and quite a few managed to desert and get out during the heavy fighting round Madrid. I suggest that the real Peplow was killed, and probably smashed up beyond recognition. Robert Tirle said his uncle had stopped a bomb. Lambrooke saw the chance of making a dash for it, swopped papers, realised that this was the moment to clear out altogether, and fetched up in the Argentine as Raymond Peplow with a valid British passport.'

'Assuming there's something in this flight of fancy of yours,' said the A.C. thoughtfully, 'why do you suppose that Lambrooke should suddenly take it into his head to come over here after an interval of thirty years, and burgle his old home?'

'So far, the only clue to that, sir,' replied Pollard frankly, 'is that a crazy thing like that's in character. He seems to have done outrageous things all the way up. You'll have seen the bit in the report about his parties over there. But what sparked him off this time's a mystery up to now.'

'You know, coincidences are really rather extraordinary sometimes. The case has made the Tirles news, of course. I ran across my younger brother yesterday. He was up at Oxford in Lambrooke's time, and started reminiscing about the chap—whom he assumes dead, naturally. He did do some quite outrageous things, such as rising up in church and forbidding the banns of a female don. He was sent down for that, and for consistently breaking every rule in the book.'

Pollard realised that he was beginning to feel excited, and firmly took himself in hand.

'If we accept the identity swop, sir,' he said, 'it brings a new element into the case: motive. Both Lord Seton and Mrs Giles Tirle had the opportunity to attack Peplow, but now it looks as though his death could have been caused deliberately, instead of being an accident arising from tackling a burglar. What if either of them recognised him? Surely they'd each got a red-hot motive for putting paid to him? Lord Seton stood to lose the title and the estate, and for Mrs Tirle it meant that her son probably wouldn't succeed.'

'Imagine it all coming out in court,' mused the A.C. 'The *cause célèbre* of the seventies... But let's face it, Pollard, it could never be proved. If Peplow was buried as an English milord, we could probably get him dug up, even though it was in Red Spain, although I blench at the prospect of the red tape. However, as he was apparently smashed to bits, a few missing teeth aren't going to be legal grounds for identification. And the autopsy X-rays of Lambrooke don't show any abnormalities, and they say the teeth fillings are quite recent. To sum up, neither set of remains is going to provide conclusive evidence of identity. Are you proposing to tackle the family, and hope that you'll startle someone into an admission of having recognised Lambrooke?'

'This is the thing, sir. I'd like to discuss it with you. Could any of them have recognised him after all this time? Beyond doubt, I mean?'

The A.C. took out his cigarette case, helped himself, and extended it to Pollard as an afterthought.

'I'm damned if I know the answer to that one,' he said, accepting a light. 'Thirty years is the whale of a long time, isn't it, and on the far side of the mental watershed of the war into the bargain? All this time the family have accepted his death as an unquestioned fact, and the chap must have practically faded from their minds. And meanwhile—if this identity swop really took place, Lambrooke's been developing into a middle-aged man who's spent getting on for the whole of his adult life in a foreign climate and culture.'

'He'd obviously have changed enormously in appearance,' Pollard said meditatively, 'and as people never imagine those who are absent as growing older, they wouldn't be prepared for the change in him. But you don't only recognise people by their faces, though. There's a chap's walk, for instance, and the way he stands.'

'A good point, that. What's your personal opinion on whether he was recognised by one or more of the family, Pollard?'

There was a pause.

'In some ways the Tirles are the hardest people to size up I've ever had to cope with,' he said at last, with apparent inconsequence. 'It's something more subtle than a professional criminal's expert lying. Difficult to put your finger on. I think it's a kind of inborn unconscious reticence to the outsider, arising from belonging to what is still a closed society to some extent. Anyway, to answer your question, sir . . . I'll take Lady Arminel Tirle first. I personally think the way Peplow was standing when she happened to look up and caught sight of him reminded her of her dead brother, and shook her a bit as these things do. But she's a robust person with plenty of commonsense, and likely to forget all about it in a short time. Then the discovery of the body the next morning would probably have brought it back to her mind, and made her feel vaguely uneasy. Then we suddenly turn up with the photograph, and she instinctively jibs at looking at it, just in case . . . It takes her a minute or two to get herself in hand again. She shrinks from the idea of recognising her brother, even while telling herself it's impossible, so she's only too ready to be put off by the unfamiliar face, and says quite honestly that the man's a complete stranger to her.'

The A.C. nodded.

'I've never met the lady, but I know the type,' he observed. 'I should think you've reconstructed soundly there. What about the sister-in-law, late of the Resistance?'

'You could say she's nearer to the professional, sir. Trained to get herself out of tight corners, and get misleading information across, as I said in my report. I'm positive she knows something, but we haven't yet established whether she ever knew Lambrooke. She didn't marry Mr Giles Tirle until after the war. Of course, she may have been up at Oxford with Lambrooke.'

'I might be able to get a line on that from my brother, to save time. Leaving her on one side for the moment, what about Seton himself?'

'He had much the best opportunity of recognising Lambrooke, sir. He went down into the priest's hole and examined the body at very close range under a powerful electric light. And he was knocked flat when I told him it wasn't an accident. But couldn't he reasonably refuse to give a positive identification? I don't really feel that it could be expected of him under the circumstances. And what is more, I'm quite sure he's sorted this out for himself: he's anything but dim-witted. By the time I saw him on Thursday morning, he was virtually back on an even keel.'

'I entirely agree with all this,' the A.C. said, stubbing out his cigarette. 'And even if we could prove that he assaulted the self-styled Peplow, we could never establish that recognition was the motive. Self-defence while tackling a burglar would be an absolutely cast-iron defence. To that extent, I'm afraid this highly ingenious idea of yours will have to go into cold storage. Don't look so hipped, Pollard. It won't be the first case shelved in default of legal proof, even if it comes to shelving it. Not worrying about your reputation, are you? What's your next move to be?'

'We're interviewing Dick White, the Emmett girl's boy-friend, down at Warhampton tomorrow, and hoping to get that loose end tied up. If we do, the only option still open for the moment is to work on possible links with the other country house robberies. Meanwhile Longman's hard at it trying to pick up the Peplow-Lambrooke trail at Heathrow.'

'All very sound, although a bit lacking in dramatic appeal compared with getting up a case against the eighth Earl. On your reckoning he's the ninth, I suppose? Well, good luck to you, and keep me posted.'

As Pollard slipped his latchkey into the lock Jane came running lightly down the stairs.

'Timed to a second,' she said indistinctly in his arms. 'Both of them potted and flat out again. Thank heaven they've stopped demanding the ten o'clock feed. Come up and have a look.'

The house was cool and quiet, and smelt of clothes airing, baby powder and roses. It's like getting out into the country after being in a noisy stinking traffic jam, Pollard thought as he followed his wife upstairs. In two small cots Andrew and Rose Pollard were deep in sleep, their faces healthily sun-burnt, and a film of red-gold hair shining on their heads. Andrew heaved a sigh of utter contentment, and thrust up a tiny clenched fist. Rose was dribbling.

'Teething's imminent,' Jane said, plying a tissue. 'They've both been stuffing their fingers into their mouths today. Let's hope for a quiet night—as far as they're concerned, I mean . . . Have you eaten, by the way?'

'Ages ago, and nauseatingly, at the canteen,' he said, releasing her.

'Come down to the kitchen, then, and I'll knock up omelettes, and we'll open a bottle of the rosé. I had some supper about eight, but I'm simply ravenous again, myself.'

Pollard carefully propped open the door of the twins' room a few inches, and went downstairs after her.

CHAPTER NINE

ON THE following morning Pollard went down to War-hampton with some reluctance, wondering if he would not have done better to hand over the job of interviewing Dick White to Toye, and concentrated on the files of the other State Home robberies himself. He felt sure that confirmation of the Emmetts' statements would be forthcoming, but little, if anything else could be expected.

The Warhampton police were interested and helpful. Pollard learnt that the Whites were a thoroughly respectable family, and that nothing at all was known to Dick's disadvantage. After a satisfactory school career he had gone into Crunchaway's, and had become a long-distance van driver.

'Clean licence, too,' added the Warhampton Chief Superintendent.

Dick White had turned up at the police headquarters on time, and was a freckled young man with a pleasant, open face, at the moment looking unnaturally worried. On being assured that Scotland Yard had no interest in the peregrinations of his van as such, he brightened up to some extent.

'Matter of fact, sir,' he told Pollard, 'I've been worried stiff, thinkin' there's somethin' I ought to pass on, an' not wantin' to get drorn in, because of the job, see?'

Pollard sat up mentally. The hunch that he'd better go to Warhampton could have been sound, after all.

'What's on your mind?' he asked. 'We won't use any of it unless we have to.'

Encouraged by this, Dick White embarked on an unexpected story. He knew the lie of the land at Brent well, having spent several holidays with the Emmetts, and had at once thought of the sandpit as the ideal place for caching the van overnight. It was approached by a rough track with a bend in it, which concealed it from a minor road at the back of Brent park. He had driven down as planned, arriving just before half-past ten on Tuesday night, run the van in, and parked her over on the right, thinking he'd turn by daylight. He had not noticed any other vehicles there, but on coming back at about twenty past five on Wednesday morning, he had been horrified to see a bad dent and scrape low down on the side of the van. He could see tyre tracks coming from behind a clump of bushes at the back of the sandpit, and there were skid marks on a patch of rough ground near the entrance. Dick snorted with indignation. He'd left masses of room for anything to pass.

'Hold on a minute,' interrupted Pollard. 'Has the damage been made good?'

'Not it. I've gotta drive around lookin' as though I can't 'andle 'er.'

Much relieved, Pollard despatched Toye to telephone Crockmouth, and ask for an immediate investigation of the sandpit, and also to get hold of a photographer. While they waited for him to come back, he questioned Dick White about his route to Brent, and in minute detail about his night at the Emmetts. The young man's account tallied with theirs in all respects. He also volunteered a statement that he hadn't slept too well, being worried about getting off the next morning, and was quite certain he would have heard anyone mucking around during the night. No, he hadn't seen a soul when he cut through the park on Tuesday night, nor the next morning. He'd tried hard to go off quietly, but Rosalie had let the wicket slam when she was saying goodbye, and they'd had a bit of a giggle, thinking Lady Arminel might take a look out.

So Mrs Giles did hear a door slam, Pollard thought. That

part of her evidence at least was true. He formed a vivid mental picture of her slipping on a dressing gown and going towards the door leading into the public rooms. What did she find? A door unlocked on the ground floor, or the panel standing open? Or even nothing untoward at all?

His reflections were cut short by the return of Toye with the Warhampton police photographer. Dick White, not looking too happy about the company he was keeping, escorted the party to the nearby Crunchaway premises. The firm worked a five-day week, and there were few people about. Vans were neatly parked in the loading yard. They were highly conspicuous, being painted overall with a design of giant golden-brown crisps and snacks, and bore the name of the firm in huge letters on back and sides. Leading the way to one of them, Dick pointed out the damage, adding gloomily that the garage foreman had created something awful about it.

After a careful inspection they all agreed that the corresponding damage on a car of average size would probably have come just below window level.

'Near side,' emphasised Dick White, 'There weren't no call to back out. Buckets o' room to turn in the pit.'

There followed careful measuring, recorded by Toye, and photography of the damaged area. Pollard then cautiously removed fragments of paint, and transferred them to a stoppered phial taken from his case.

'We'll get the boys at the Yard on to these right away,' he said. 'It could give us the colour of the car.'

'There's a microscope back at the station, sir,' the photographer told him hopefully. 'You might care to have a look yourself?'

This suggestion was duly carried out. Pollard finally straightened up, detaching himself from the eyepiece.

'What do you make of it?' he asked.

The man subjected the material to an intense scrutiny.

'I'd say the bash was done by a car with lightish grey paintwork,' he said at last. 'Smoke grey's the trade name

E

of the shade, I think.'

'I agree,' said Pollard. 'This was a useful idea of yours: it'll save time. I'm going to put Crockmouth on to a medium-sized light grey car.'

When he returned from a conversation with Inspector Diplock, he found that Toye had finished typing Dick White's statement. The young man was reading it through, looking depressed.

'Brace up,' Pollard adjured him. 'You know, it's a hundred to one that the car which biffed your van had a necking couple on board, and was nothing whatever to do with our case. Do you agree that this statement's a fair record of what you've told us?'

'It's fair enough,' Dick White replied, signing his name in a large round hand. 'Better keep me fingers crossed that it don't have to come out, though. Job suits me, and they aren't all that easy to come by. Rosalie and me want to get married in the spring, what's more.'

After further reassurance from Pollard, and undertakings to put in a word with the firm if necessary, he went off, looking on the whole relieved. Half an hour later the Yard men managed to extricate themselves, having had a hasty snack on trays in the Chief Superintendent's office, and caught an early afternoon train back to London.

It was far from full, and they secured a compartment to themselves.

'Don't kid yourself that all these developments mean we're getting anywhere,' Pollard remarked, subsiding into his corner. 'We're just reducing the list of possible suspects. The Emmetts' ten p.m. caller can be crossed off the list now. So what?'

'There's the grey car,' replied Toye, taking this rhetorical question at its face value. 'Could be that Peplow had another chap with him after all. And there's the chance of a link-up with these other robberies.'

He glanced at his briefcase which contained one of the files which they had brought with them to read through in the train.

'Glutton for work, aren't you? Here, chuck over my case. I suppose we may as well take a look at the stuff; it's about the only line open to us at the moment.'

The police officers in charge of the enquiries, however, had carried them out exhaustively. As the train began to run through the outer suburbs of London, Toye remarked that the chaps seemed to have gone to town on the job, and got nowhere.

'The only hope is to make a detailed analysis of the findings of the whole lot,' Pollard replied, stuffing a file back into his briefcase. 'I'll have a go at home tomorrow. You can do with some time off. We needn't go down to Crockmouth till lateish.'

This programme was duly carried out. On Sunday morning, while Jane and the Italian au pair occupied themselves with domestic ploys, Pollard withdrew to the dining room, and proceeded to cover the table with heaps of typescript. He then took a large sheet of paper, ruled columns, and thought out a series of headings such as House, Owner, Date of Robbery, Objects Stolen, Insurance, Methods Employed, Distance From London, Open To Public? The last and widest column he headed comprehensively Remarks. He then worked systematically at transferring all the known facts about the five robberies and the attempted one at Brent from the files to his columns. Finally he settled down to consider his data.

Jane, coming in just before twelve, remarked that it looked like a school timetable in the making.

'Very definitely Stately,' she said, reading over his shoulder. 'Wonbridge Castle, Sir Matthew Dent. Coin collection. Corridon Manor. The Hon. Mrs James Crabtree. Two small icons. I'm not quite so sure about Mr S. Rothstein of Yarndown House and his Chinese jade, though . . . Are you getting anywhere?'

'Not really,' he said, stretching. 'It's obvious that the jobs are all run from a base in London. They're all within easy driving distance. All the stuff lifted is relatively small and possible to carry off on the person, and none of it has turned up, as far as we know. Three of the houses are open to the public, and in each of these the thief seems to have gone in as a visitor and managed to hide till the place was closed for the night. In the others there was forced entry through a very cleverly chosen weak spot. All this suggests detailed previous knowledge of the ground. But as for making useful deductions from all this—nil. The only thing to do is to go on hopefully combing the blasted files, I suppose.'

'The significant thing probably isn't in them at all,' Jane said. 'That's how it would be in a detective novel. Then the sleuth gets a blinding flash of inspiration in his bath, and in the last chapter a colleague draws him aside and mutters about promotion rumours. Listen to your son yelling with hunger and rage. Are you coming to help spoon in veal dinners? Mariella's off at twelve today. I thought we'd eat in peace later, when the children are fed.'

Pollard thankfully abandoned the files and joined the family party in the kitchen. He was allotted Rose, as being slightly more amenable than her brother. At first she concentrated on her food intake, but soon began to watch Andrew, and imitate his attempts to grab the spoon. A sudden coup landed a dollop of veal dinner in Pollard's face. His anguished exclamation was greeted with delighted crowing from the twins.

'They're ganging up on us already,' he remarked as he mopped. 'Didn't you see them exchange meaning glances?'

After lunch and coffee in the garden he went back to the analysis. It was a hot afternoon, and the somnolent droning of bees came drifting in at the open windows. Another unproductive hour went by, and he became depressed by the feeling that he must be flogging a dead horse. Presently his ears caught the clinking of china, and he got up and looked out of the window. The twins had woken up from their afternoon sleep, and were lying on a rug under a tree, attired only in nappies. They were working their arms and legs energetically, pausing at intervals to take note of each other's existence, and gaze up at the green tracery overhead. Going into the kitchen he found Jane filling the teapot, and picked up the tray.

Some time later the summer afternoon was shattered by the ringing of the telephone.

'Blast and damn,' Pollard said, heaving himself out of a deck chair, and going towards the house.

As he had expected, it was a call from the Yard. A Mr George Snell was demanding to see the officer in charge of the Brent case, and refusing to talk to anyone else.

'Another crackpot, you can bet your bottom dollar. What's made you ring me about him?'

'He says he's just flown in from Buenos Aires, sir. We rang Heathrow, and his name was on a Pan Am passenger list.'

'OK,' said Pollard, feeling slightly taken aback. 'I'll be along. Get hold of Sergeant Toye, will you?'

As he returned to the garden Jane raised her eyebrows, indicating resignation.

'I suppose we must be thankful for small mercies,' she remarked. 'It's been a good day up to now. What is it?'

He told her.

'I've got a feeling this could be important,' she said, beginning to stack the tea things. 'It's all right, you know. I realised life would be like this when I married you. Suppose you'd just been ordered to Vietnam? Bring them in for me, will you? I'll take the tray.'

Pollard stooped to gather up a twin under each arm, and carried them carefully into the house. Andrew fought furiously. Rose appeared to find the experience amusing.

Pollard's first impression of George Snell was favourable. He found a middle-aged man of above average height, a rugged weatherbeaten face, and keen blue eyes. His manner of speech was slow and deliberate, and Pollard fancied he could detect a westcountry drawl under the transatlantic twang. Not another crackpot, if I'm any judge of a chap, he decided, during preliminary general conversation. He learnt that George Snell had first gone out to the Argentine after the war on an engineering contract, and liked the life so much that he had worked there ever since.

'It's the climate and the crowds get me down back here,' he said. 'You kinda feel you can't breathe. Not here in London, anyway. I expect I'll be back when I start cracking up, all the same. Maybe you'll care to take a look at these.'

He passed over a British passport and a professional card describing him as a consultant engineer.

'Thanks,' said Pollard, returning them. 'Well, Mr Snell, you've come a long way, and it can't be a cheap trip, either. Do I take it you've something to tell us about Raymond Peplow? By the way, you mayn't know that we've found out that Raymond Peplow wasn't his real name.'

'Yeah, I know,' replied George Snell. 'The English papers get flown out these days. But let's call him that, or we'll get snarled up.' He paused, and stared fixedly at some object on the top of Pollard's desk. 'You've got Peplow wrong, you guys here,' he said abruptly. 'He wasn't a crook, and he wasn't running with 'em, either. You can take it from me.'

'No?' queried Pollard. 'Then how do you explain the fact that he was found in hiding at Brent, in a room full of valuables, with housebreaking kit on him?'

There was a lengthy pause.

'There was a bet,' George Snell said heavily. 'I guess Peplow's death's on me.'

Pollard's immediate reaction was exasperation. He's a crank after all, he thought impatiently. He was on the point of speaking when he caught sight of the expression on the other's face, and checked himself.

'Hadn't you better begin at the beginning?' he suggested. 'How long had you known Peplow?'

The story came out slowly, but coherently. The two men

had chanced to meet soon after George Snell had first gone out to the Argentine. At first he had regarded Peplow with the contempt of a fighting man for someone who'd managed to dodge the call-up to the armed forces. Then, after a bit, he'd come to realise that whatever Peplow's motives had been, he was no coward or cissie, and hadn't stayed out of it to line his pockets while other chaps took the rap.

'He was an anti-war guy. A genuine one. Most of 'em kid themselves, but he was OK.'

'I suppose you got to know him well over the years?' prompted Pollard.

'Depends what you mean by well. Better than anybody else out there, but we weren't buddies. He was an odd chap, old Peppy. Kept himself to himself, and clear of women, except on a strictly business footing. But he was real good company when he felt that way. We had some swell times together. We took some trips camping in the Cordilleras and up in the Chaco, hunting and fishing. He didn't have any use for the stuffed shirt parties the British colony put on, any more than I do. My old man was a gas fitter.'

'What about Peplow's old man?' Pollard asked, watching George Snell keenly.

'I wouldn't know. He never talked about his people, or why he'd come out, and I never asked. It wasn't my business. Maybe that's why we got on. Mind you, he was class. You can't miss it. But he sure had it in for the stuffed shirts. I figured he'd cut loose.'

'What about politics? Had he extreme Leftist views?'

'Not he. Red—Black—Big Business—he said the boss class was the same the world over, and he hated its guts.'

Pollard considered.

'Mr Snell,' he said, 'I'm not contesting what you've told me, but it doesn't altogether tally with what we've learnt from the authorities. For instance, he seems to have made quite a nice bit of money, and qualified for the boss class himself, to some extent. Then you say he was a lone wolf, and couldn't do with ordinary conventional social life. We understand that he entertained in quite a big way at times.'

George Snell flung himself back in his chair, folded his arms, and stared straight at Pollard.

'This is it. Peplow didn't add up. It sometimes seemed to me he'd never properly grown up, either, in some ways. Don't get me wrong. He was on the spot, for sure. You've only got to look at some of his deals. But he'd kick out at things like a teenager. Things like stuffed shirts, and armaments, and underdogs anywhere. And yet he'd throw a swell party to the manner born. Stag parties, mostly, ending up with the chaps getting a bit high, and daft bets being made. Nearly led to trouble, some of 'em.'

'Was the bet you mentioned just now one of these?'

'Yeah. I'll blame myself for the rest of my life. Not that I ever thought he'd taken me seriously.'

George Snell relapsed into silence.

'How did Brent come into it? It's a pretty far cry.'

'I'll tell you, and I'm dam' glad I've got proof in writing. About six weeks back I came on Peplow looking at a British magazine. It was an advertising stunt, to get tourists over here. A posh glossy affair, full of pictures. He showed me a big piece about this place Brent, and this earl chap it belongs to, and how you could go in for five bob a time, and see round the house and garden. There was a lot about the swell pictures, and a sort of locket which Charles the Second had given to the family, with a picture of himself inside. It seemed OK to me if you like that sort of thing, but Peplow blew his top. He went on about it being a scandal, and that the poor had paid for the place being put up, hundreds of years ago, and now they were being fooled into paying to keep it going. A bloody racket, he called it, and a lot more. I got fed up with him in the end, and told him to belt up, and come and have a drink. I never thought any more about it until he threw a dinner for a crowd of us a week or two later. We sure made a night of it, and on the way home—he was giving me a lift as my bus was in dock—he'd got to the arguing stage. He'd tried to get some of the chaps to stage a hold-up, just for the hell of it. They'd cried off, and he went on about people's lack of guts all the way back in the car, and how he'd take on any bet offered him, anytime. I said I'd bet him a hundred quid he wouldn't go over and pinch that locket he'd been bellyaching about, and suggested he could sell it to a fence, and give the cash to Oxfam. I was a bit sozzled myself, come to that, but I swear I only meant it as a joke, or thought he'd take it as anything else, once he'd sobered up.'

'What was the next development?' Pollard asked.

'I went off first thing next morning to a site a thousand miles down south, and didn't come back for ten days. When I showed up again, I heard Peplow'd flown to London on a business trip. I wasn't all that surprised. He'd been launching out into tourist hotel sites. Then I got this, postmarked here a week ago today.'

Pollard took the air letter held out to him. It was merely headed London, and consisted of only a few lines. The writer had had a good trip over, and would be flying back by the end of the week. There followed some pithy remarks about changes for the worse in Britain. Finally, George Snell was advised to watch the English papers for the disappearance of an historic object from a Stately Home. The letter was signed R.P.

'Even then, I took it for granted he was kidding. Keeping up the joke we'd had that night.'

'I'll have to ask you to leave this with us,' Pollard said. 'I'll give you a receipt, of course. If it's genuine—and I'm not suggesting it isn't—it confirms what you've just told me. We can check the handwriting with the signature on the passport.'

'OK by me,' George Snell replied wearily. 'It's genuine, all right. Say, I'd like to see old Peplow put away decently. What's the drill?'

'The resumed inquest's tomorrow, down at Crockmouth. There'll be legal complications, of course, because of the fresh information about identity, but there's no doubt that the coroner will issue a burial certificate, and as there are no relatives, an offer from you to make the funeral arrangements would certainly be accepted.'

'I guess I'll come along, then, and try to get it fixed up for Tuesday, if folk can move that fast back here. Maybe I'll take a look at this dump Brent. Say, are you guys going to get the chap that did poor old Peppy?'

'I hope so,' said Pollard gravely. 'Mr Snell, I don't think you should blame yourself for what happened.'

'Thanks a lot,' George Snell replied. 'I wish I could feel that way myself.'

He turned and looked at Toye who was emerging from the back of the room with his notebook.

'Say, will all this have to come out in evidence tomorrow?'

'No,' Pollard told him. 'You'll certainly be asked to give evidence of identity, and I'm afraid that'll mean viewing the body, but we shall then ask for a further adjournment, which I'm sure will be granted in view of the very unusual circumstances.'

George Snell's unexpected appearance and its repercussions delayed the start for Crockmouth, but even so the Sunday evening traffic on the roads was heavy, and the journey a slow one. Although irritated by hold-ups, petrol fumes and the constant stream of passing cars on the upstream side of the road, Pollard was glad of a chance to do some uninterrupted thinking on the way down.

A Yard handwriting expert had unhesitatingly pronounced that the signature on the Raymond Peplow passport and the air letter received by George Snell had been written by the same hand. Officially, of course, the acceptance of the letter's evidence awaited confirmation of his bona fides, and his relations with Peplow, but Pollard found that he had no doubt whatever of its validity. So one more piece of the jigsaw had slipped into position. Not that it helped much, if at all, in the search for the killer. Or did it, perhaps, by making the Peplow/Lambrooke identity swop even more credible, turn one's thoughts to the Tirles again? To Lord Seton with his indisputable know-how, or to the formidable Mrs Giles Tirle?

Pollard shifted his position, made a caustic remark to Toye about a driver who overtook them just below a blind crest, and settled down to his thinking once more.

The grounds on which he had decided that Lord Seton and Mrs Tirle were above suspicion still held good. So, too, did his conviction that Emmett was not the assailant, although he might conceivably have been bribed to let someone in and/or out. Dick White was obviously in the clear. It was all so very negative, but on the other hand, negative conclusions about all the known suspects must surely point clearly to X, the Person Unknown? But then mustn't X somehow tie up with Peplow-Lambrooke, and so far not the faintest trace of any connection had come to light.

As they approached Crockmouth, he summarised the results of his meditations to Toye, and found that the latter, a rather slow but very pertinacious thinker, had arrived at much the same point.

'It's gone stale on us with this endless chewing over,' he remarked, 'We could do with a shot in the arm.'

They were to get one with unexpected rapidity. On arriving at the police station they were triumphantly informed that the trail of a grey Austin Princess with a scrape on her near side had been picked up.

CHAPTER TEN

IN THE cold light of day the news of the damaged grey car seemed less exhilarating. Inspector Diplock explained that after getting Pollard's call from Warhampton, he had immediately alerted the local force throughout the area, and ordered enquiries to be made. An enterprising Crockmouth constable had thought of one Henry Tubbs, a pensioner who frequented the town's large free car park in the hopes of picking up tips from motorists for small services. He was known to be perfectly honest, so the police were accustomed to turn a blind eye to this practice. In reply to questions Tubbs had stated without hesitation that there had been a grey Austin with a nasty bash on her near side in the car park on Wednesday morning. He clearly remembered seeing it at about ten-thirty. Asked why he had noticed it particularly, he replied that it was badly parked, right over the white line, stopping somebody else getting in. The loss of a potential employer had obviously rankled with him. No, he hadn't taken its number. He wasn't a cop, nor yet a dratted boy with a notebook, running all over the park and getting in people's way. Finally the constable extracted the information that the car had gone when Tubbs returned from his dinner, at just on two, and he hadn't seen it since.

Pollard congratulated Inspector Diplock on being so quick off the mark, and highly commended the constable. He learnt that further enquiries were being energetically pursued, but so far, unfortunately, without result. The inspection of the sandpit had confirmed Dick White's statement in every respect. Casts had been taken of the two sets of tyre tracks, and the ground had also been carefully photographed. A few drops of oil behind a big clump of brambles where the grey car had been hidden, suggested that it had not stood there for any great length of time.

'If it turns out to be anything to do with us,' Pollard said, 'that fits in with the probable timing: between just after nine-forty, when those phone calls were made, and midnight, which Dr Netley obviously thinks is the latest time of death.'

He hurried off to the conference with the Chief Constable, which Superintendent Perry had been unable to ward off any longer.

It began inauspiciously, Major Egerton appearing to feel that the initially wrong identification of the body found at Brent was in some way a reflection on his men, and Pollard had to use all his tact to convince him that this was not the case. He then embarked on the evidence provided by George Snell, but without touching on the question of Peplow's real identity. Major Egerton listened incredulously.

'Preposterous!' he snorted. 'Of course a chap who'd skulk out there while decent men were fighting for their country would do anything. This Snell seems a pretty rum customer, too. Glad to hear you're checking up on him. Still, you say your handwriting wallah says the chap who signed the Peplow passport wrote the air letter. We don't want any of this coming out until you've heard from the Argentine people. We'd better see Richardson again about the further adjournment. About this car, now.'

Pollard gave a résumé of his visit to Warhampton, and Superintendent Perry an account of the findings in the sandpit.

'I think all this rules out young White,' Pollard said. 'And in my own mind I'm certain Emmett wasn't directly responsible for Peplow's death. If he was fixed to lock up after somebody, well, there must have been two men on the job, and the other one went for Peplow, and could have been the driver of this car we're looking for. Smart work of that constable of yours to pick up its trail so quickly. Do you think there's anything to be gained by broadening the search area? I don't want a broadcast appeal yet: it'll only put the chap on his guard, if he's really our man.'

'Lull him into a false sense of security, eh?' suggested the Chief Constable picturesquely. 'Yes, we can step things up with our neighbours. We'll get on to that right away. See to it, Perry, will you?'

Realising that he was about to tread on dangerous ground, Pollard broached the subject of alternative suspects.

'You know, sir,' he said. 'I find this idea of the second chap difficult to swallow, although we've obviously got to consider it carefully, and follow up this car clue. What would have been Peplow's idea in bringing somebody along with him? He could perfectly well have carried through the robbery on his own.'

The Chief Constable subjected him to a penetrating stare.

'Have you formed an alternative theory, then?'

'Nothing so definite. But I'm bound to take note of the fact that, quite apart from Emmett, Lord Seton and Mrs Giles Tirle had access to the miniatures room that night. On paper it's possible that one of them heard a noise or saw a light in the room, went to investigate, was threatened by Peplow, and accidentally killed him in self-defence. It's a situation lending itself to panic moves.'

'You can't be serious, Pollard!' The Chief Constable stared at him in stupefaction. 'Seton panic? It'd take a dam' sight more than accidentally killing a burglar to rattle him. I should have thought it was obvious. As to Felicity Tirle, have you ever seen a woman trying to kick a football? Enough to make a cat laugh! It's out of the question that a woman's involved. And if she were the panicking sort she'd be dead, let me tell you. She worked in the Resistance in Occupied France.'

'I entirely agree with what you say, sir,' Pollard replied,

making mental reservations with regard to Felicity Tirle's physical capabilities. 'I merely said that it was a theoretical possibility, and as such, we had to consider it. So we come back to this inexplicable second chap, and at the moment our only lead is the car.'

'Quite,' said Major Egerton, recovering himself. 'Well, you can count on us to go all out. We'd better be getting along to the inquest.'

The coroner's court was not large, and already packed to suffocation point. As Pollard slipped into one of the seats kept for the police he caught a glimpse of Lord Seton, accompanied by Robert Tirle, and wished that he were better placed to observe the former.

It was soon clear that members of the public who had hoped for a morning of sensational disclosures were again doomed to disappointment. Discussion of the legal implications of the problem of the deceased's identity dragged on interminably. The only flicker of interest arose from the appearance of George Snell in the witness box. He made a good impression, stating without any hesitation that the body he had just viewed was that of the man he had known for over twenty years in the Argentine as Raymond Peplow, and that he had no knowledge of the deceased's real name. Asked by the coroner if he had known in advance of the deceased's trip to England, he replied in the negative. He himself had been away in connection with his work, and on his return had gathered that it was a business trip in connection with a real estate deal. On hearing of the disaster at Brent, he had anticipated a projected visit to England to see if he could be of any assistance. Yes, he would describe himself as a friend of the deceased's, although not a very close one.

To Pollard's relief George Snell was permitted to stand down, and the enquiry moved on to the medical evidence as to the cause of death. This mainly took the form of an exhaustive statement by Dr Netley. At last the coroner announced himself prepared to issue a burial certificate,

George Snell's offer to be responsible for the funeral was accepted, and the police request for a further adjournment of a month granted.

When Pollard was able to extract himself he saw George Snell besieged by newsmen, but apparently holding his own successfully.

'Let's beat it,' he said to Toye. 'Diplock's going to see if he wants any help over the funeral arrangements. I could do with some grub. We'll just look in to see if anything's come through about that car.'

There was no further news. Over lunch Pollard realised that the case had reached a stage which he always detested and found exceedingly trying: that of inactive waiting for results from enquiries being carried out by other people. For the moment there *was* nothing to do beyond the endless chewing over of stale facts.

'We'll go over and have a look at the sandpit ourselves,' he said suddenly over coffee.

The expedition was unrewarding, however, beyond confirming all the information gathered by Inspector Diplock and his men. Pollard had noted the absence of houses along the road as they approached from the direction of Crockmouth. On coming out of the sandpit they walked in the opposite direction, and found none there either. To the south of the minor road stretched the park of Brent, and open fields lay to the north.

'No hope of anybody having heard a car start up,' he remarked.

They paused at a padlocked gate leading into the park, and leant on it, resting their arms on the topmost bar. The sky had clouded over, and the great house loomed forbiddingly. A surprising amount of activity was in evidence. Rows of coaches and cars were visible in the car park, and a constantly changing crowd could be seen round the tea room and the shop.

'Cashing in, from the look of things,' Toye remarked.

'They'll soon make up for the closure,' Pollard agreed.

He wondered how Lady Seton was making out under the continuing strain, and if there were still delphiniums in the fireplace of the great hall. He stared at the house. How many furtive approaches had been made to it under cover of darkness in the course of its long history? Peripatetic priests in the first Elizabeth's day. King's men, and perhaps Parliament men during the Civil War. Even Charles himself on the way to the Channel coast after Worcester, with a price on his head, but still not in too much of a hurry to forego a spot of dalliance with the lady of the house...

'Come on,' he said, rousing himself. 'We'd better go back. If nothing's turned up we'll take an hour or two off.'

The Yard had telephoned confirmation received of George Snell's authenticity and relations with Peplow, but there was no news of the wanted car. Toye went off to a cinema, which was showing one of his favourite westerns, and Pollard set off on a solitary walk to the far end of Windle Point, on the east side of Crockmouth Bay. He soon left the holiday crowds behind, and entered a grey solitude of sea and sky. Arriving at his destination he dropped on to his stomach, and crawled forward to a spot from which he could gaze down on the surging waves far below without a sense of vertigo. Slowly and relentlessly they were demolishing the great rocky bastion. A weak place had been discovered and tunnelled through, forming a natural arch under which the white foam came thundering in rhythmic bursts. After a time the swirl of the water, reiterated by the wheeling of the gulls overhead, became hypnotic... Roused by a maniac scream in his ear, he looked at his watch. He had slept for over an hour. Hastily scrambling to his feet, he started back to the town.

There he learnt that the funeral could not be held before Wednesday, and that no reports of a damaged grey car had come in.

The evening and the following morning dragged interminably, divided between further unproductive brooding over the files of the robberies, and the continual reviewing of the pros and cons of issuing an appeal for information about the car on the air and in the Press. Inspector Diplock was strongly in favour of this.

'Trouble is, the whole place is lousy with cars this time of year,' he said. 'Why, even the filling stations just bung in the juice without hardly looking at you and hustle you off to make room at the pump for the chap on your tail. Don't even try to sell you some gadget or other.'

'If nothing's turned up by tonight,' Pollard said, suddenly coming to a decision, 'we'll run up to the Yard, and get something out on a nation-wide basis.'

The afternoon crawled like the morning. This time Toye accompanied Pollard on the walk out to Windle Point. For most of the way they strode along in silence, conversational topics exhausted. It was heavily overcast and sultry, with thunderclouds building up on the far horizon.

As they returned to the town and were walking along the seafront, they ran into George Snell outside the Hotel Magnificent. He greeted them with obvious pleasure, and invited them in for a drink.

'I sure need one,' he said, as they sank into chairs in an opulent lounge. 'Going all round this place Brent this afternoon put me in mind of a ride I once took on the New York subway in the rush hour.' He broke off to order drinks from a waiter. 'Boy, oh boy,' he continued, 'was there a crowd? The cops've got a chap on point duty out there.'

'It won't last like this,' Pollard told him. 'Some other place will hit the headlines, and draw off the sensation-seekers.'

George Snell, however, was clearly impressed by the profit potential of Brent.

'I'll grant you there's a boom right now,' he said, 'but I figure that set-up more than earns its keep the way they've got everything lined up. I've been backstage. Young Tirle took me round the whole place: house, grounds, tea place, market garden—the lot. Nice lad. Nothing upstage about him.'

Pollard looked his surprise.

'Young Robert Tirle? How did he get on to you?'

'Came up and spoke to me after the inquest. Nice friendly young chap. He was interested in Peplow, and what'd made him pick on Brent. I told him about the magazine article. Kept quiet about that damn bet, of course. Then he said he'd show me round if I cared to turn up. So I hired a car and went along. The driver told me the place was a gold mine, with so many people going on holiday these days. No competition anywhere near, he said.'

Without being able to pinpoint the reason for it Pollard was aware of being alerted. Puzzled, he groped in his mind without result, while continuing the conversation with George Snell.

'Are you staying over here long?' he asked.

'Coupla weeks, just to look up my folk down in Devon. I'm hiring a self-drive car from a garage the hotel's put me on to.'

Their talk flowed on easily, and a second round of drinks was ordered. At last Pollard felt that he could decently make a move, and after arranging to meet George Snell after the funeral on the following morning, emerged once more on to the seafront with Toye.

Crockmouth seemed strangely deserted, and he realised that most of the visitors must be having the early evening meal of the smaller hotels and the boarding houses. The empty beach looked dreary. He reflected that it ought always to be sunny at the seaside, and slumped down into a deck chair.

'Let's park here for a bit,' he said. 'It's stifling. I don't feel like eating yet, do you?'

'Not me,' replied Toye. 'Feels like an outside thunder-storm cooking up. Shall I ring the station, sir, just in case? There's a kiosk across the road.'

'Better, I suppose.'

A few minutes later Toye returned, and shook his head briefly. They relapsed into silence.

'Funny thing,' Pollard said presently. 'Something Snell said rang a bell. It didn't click with you, too, did it?'

'Was it to do with Brent?' Toye asked, a puzzled expression on his pale, serious face. 'Or about Peplow?'

'I can't remember—that's the trouble. Let's see if we can piece the conversation together. For some reason it's bothering me.'

Bit by bit they reconstructed what had been said. The crowds at Brent had been discussed, and the chap on point duty mentioned.

'Young Tirle,' interrupted Pollard. 'This isn't it, but doesn't it seem odd that Robert Tirle made a dead set at Snell? He's a bright lad. Can he possibly have his suspicions that Peplow was really his uncle?'

'I wouldn't think it's likely,' Toye said, after consideration. 'Wouldn't you expect a young chap of his age to show a bit of curiosity, seeing what's happened?'

'Perhaps you're right. Where did we leave off? I know. Snell said he'd hired a car and gone out to Brent.'

'That's it. And the driver said the Tirles were on to a gold mine, and there was no competition—'

He broke off as Pollard uttered a strangled exclamation, and brought his right hand down on his knee.

'That's it!' he almost shouted. "*No competition!* Now, where did we hear that before? I've got it, Toye! It was Lord Seton's secretary, last Thursday morning.' In his excitement he swung round, gripping the back of the chair. 'Remember? She was in a tiz because there was a chance that a rival show might be starting up in the neighbourhood. Then that professional adviser chap came in with Lord Seton, the one they'd had at Brent. He'd been to see this other place. Whitesisters, that's what it's called! The chap's name was Corden, from some firm called Stately Homes Limited. Then they went on talking as if nothing in the world mattered except opening these bloody great houses to the public.'

'I remember all right,' said Toye, looking baffled. 'Then the consultant fellow said Whitesisters wasn't on, didn't he?'

'Yes, he did. After all, I don't think it adds up to anything. Or does it? I'm not sure. Toye, if Corden had decided the place was no go, he must have spent some time there. When did he get there?'

Toye blinked.

'Meaning he might have slept there Tuesday night?'

'This is it. If he did, could he have slipped out and gone over to Brent, either to join up with Peplow/Lambrooke, or even to break in on his own?'

At this Toye looked reproving.

'Pretty hefty coincidence, two separate break-ins in the same night.'

'Never mind about that,' said Pollard impatiently. 'Let's focus on Corden. Professionally he gets first-class opportunities of finding out everything about these houses and what's in 'em. Why, man, the owners pay him for coming along and going over the place with a toothcomb. Don't tell me that a smart chap couldn't find a chance of taking impressions of keys while he was on the job. Now then, when I was doing that analysis of the robberies I noticed that two of the houses besides Brent had employed Stately Homes. One had some other firm, and two haven't opened ... Wait a bit, though. What a nit I am—of course, he could perfectly well have vetted them, and advised against opening!'

'Like Whitesisters?' By now Toye was showing unusual excitement. 'And the one who had the other firm, well, could be the owner didn't agree his place wasn't worth opening, and called in somebody else.'

'You're dead right. Or even taken a scunner at Corden—I did myself—and paid his consultation fee, and then gone elsewhere. Toye, do you see what all this is leading up to? If the damaged car is Corden's, he must have come down on Tuesday, but not to Whitesisters, surely? How could he have got back there during the night without his car? It was in that car park on Wednesday morning. Did he spend Tuesday night—or what was left of it—in Crockmouth, and then pick up the car again, and go on to Whitesisters on Wednesday? We've got to go out there, and find out when he turned up, and what car he was using. And, of course, get on to the Yard to find out what car he owns. Could he have hired one to come down? Here, come on. We can't stick around speculating all night.'

After the stagnation of the past few days Pollard felt revitalised. At the police station he put through his call to the Yard, and then asked Inspector Diplock to brief him on Whitesisters and its owners. He learnt that General Ormiston was a real gentleman of the old school. Retired now, and well on in his sixties. The family had owned the place for generations, but rumour had it that the General was up against it, with costs rising all the time. He was struggling to keep things going for his grandson, a boy at school. His son had been killed in a car smash a couple of years back: a terrible blow to the old people. Thinking of opening Whitesisters to the public, was he? Inspector Diplock thought this would be a doubtful proposition, Brent being the sort of set-up it was, and doing so well. Whitesisters was a nice enough place, but not in the same class.

'I'm on to something that'll probably fizzle out,' Pollard told him. 'Tell you about it when we get back.'

Toye had been studying a map, and they took the coast road running westward from Crockmouth in the direction of Wythe Bay. About four miles out of the town they branched right over a ridge on to a secondary road. This followed a valley roughly parallel to the coast. The road rose gently as they passed through a succession of villages.

'It's about a mile beyond this one,' Toye said. 'Steepleford, it's called.'

Rather a claustrophobic valley, Pollard thought, unless it was just the oppressive evening. The trees were absolutely motionless, dark and solid in their heavy July foliage. The road curved slightly to the left, and Whitesisters suddenly loomed up, sited like Brent at the foot of a wooded ridge. Whatever the religious house from which it derived its name had been like, the present building was late Georgian, slightly top-heavy in appearance and surmounted by a stone balustrade. The approach was by way of a long drive in need of resurfacing, which ran through an unkempt-looking park.

'They'd never get coaches in this way,' Toye said, negotiating a narrow wooden bridge.

'Might be another entrance, I suppose. The general effect's a bit down at heel, isn't it? Unless there's some pretty hot stuff inside, I'm inclined to agree with Corden about the place.'

Their reception bore out these first impressions. General Ormiston was a tall, distinguished-looking man, with the beginnings of a stoop and a worried expression. Mrs Ormiston had a faded prettiness, and a determined brightness of manner. Drinks were offered and accepted. They sat in a splendid room which called for handsome furnishings, but the carpet was worn and faded, and the curtains at the fine windows shabby.

Pollard apologised for the lateness of his call.

'As I told you over the telephone, sir, Sergeant Toye and I are working on the Brent case. At the moment we're interested in the movements of a grey Austin car which was in this part of the world last week. You'll understand that I can't be more specific. It's been reported that a car of this type was seen on this valley road on several occasions, and we felt it was possible that you or Mrs Ormiston might have noticed it. We're looking for responsible confirmation, you see.'

The slightly puzzled expressions on the Ormistons' faces cleared.

'I'm afraid you've come out on a wild goose chase,' the General told him. 'There certainly was a grey Austin—a

Princess—about here in the middle of last week, but not the one you're after. It belonged to a guest of ours.'

Pollard registered humorous resignation.

'We're quite hardened to finding ourselves barking up the wrong tree,' he said. 'The trouble is there are so many Austins around. I wonder if there could possibly have been a second one? When exactly was your visitor here, sir?'

'Let me see. He got here just before lunch on Wednesday, didn't he, dear?'

'Yes, at about a quarter to one,' Mrs Ormiston agreed. 'I remember I was beginning to hope he wouldn't be late, because of lunch getting overcooked.'

'Wednesday,' repeated Pollard with slight emphasis. 'One of our reports spoke of a grey Austin on the road on Tuesday.'

'Then if it's correct, there must have been a second one,' said General Ormiston. 'Our guest arrived for lunch on Wednesday, and left after tea on Thursday.'

'About what time would that have been?' queried Pollard.

'I can tell you exactly.' Mrs Ormiston smiled at him brightly. 'He drove off at five minutes to five. We were due at friends on the other side of Crockmouth for drinks at six, and I was beginning to wonder how we were going to make it. Dear me, that sounds dreadfully inhospitable, doesn't it? Actually it wasn't quite like having a guest in the ordinary sense of the word.'

'To tell you the truth,' General Ormiston said, refilling Pollard's glass, 'we'd asked a chap to come down and look over the place with a view to opening it to the public. Not what one would choose, but in these hard times . . . He was the same fellow the Setons had: Corden, of Stately Homes Limited.'

'That was really the trouble about the time,' Mrs Ormiston explained. 'You see, when we heard about this terrible affair at Brent, Mr Corden felt he must run over and have a word with poor Lord Seton. He went on Thursday morning, and that delayed him over finishing up here. He'd meant to leave after lunch.'

'Ah,' exclaimed Pollard. 'That explains the reports of the car being seen on Thursday morning.'

Both the Ormistons started to speak at once.

'Can't even allow you that, I'm afraid,' said the General, winning by a short head. 'Corden didn't go in his own car. It had sprung a puncture during the night. My wife lent him her little runabout. It's a black Ford Anglia.'

Concealing his interest, Pollard started on another tack.

'Would it have been possible for Mr Corden's car to have been taken out during the night without his knowledge or yours?' he asked.

The Ormistons were emphatic that it would have been quite impossible. The car had been garaged in the old stables, and would have had to have been driven round the house under the bedroom windows.

'And it's so beautifully quiet here at night,' Mrs Ormiston assured him, 'that I wake if a car drives along the valley road.'

To Pollard's satisfaction, it was suggested that they should go and have a look at the lie of the land. He noted that the police car was drawn up with its offside next to the portico of the house, and that Corden could have parked in the stable with the near side of his car close up against a wall.

The rear of Whitesisters was even more depressing than the approach from the road, consisting of a series of outbuildings in various stages of dilapidation.

'Whole lot ought to come down,' the General said. 'It's impossible to keep 'em in repair. Demolition costs the earth, that's the problem. We don't use more than a couple of 'em these days.'

'Still,' Mrs Ormiston said almost gaily, 'I'm sure something will come from Mr Corden's visit. He took infinite pains, you know, going into everything, inside and out.'

'I expect you find staffing a problem?' Pollard asked, as they walked back to the house.

'Staffing is an overstatement where we're concerned,'

replied General Ormiston. 'We're reduced to one old boy who helps with the garden, and a couple of daily women. All non-resident, of course. They come up from the village.'

'Jim Doubleday gets through a surprising amount, though,' insisted Mrs Ormiston. 'He can turn his hand to almost anything, too, which is so useful. He changed Mr Corden's wheel for him, for instance.'

After chatting for a few minutes longer Pollard thanked the Ormistons for their hospitality and help, and joined Toye in the car.

'*Sic transit gloria*,' he remarked. 'The end of an epoch. It's all right: I'm just blethering. Now for Jim Doubleday, who changed Mr Corden's wheel.'

They had unusual luck in Steepleford. On drawing up to enquire of an elderly man where Mr Jim Doubleday lived, they were informed that Doubleday was the name, and what could their informant do for the gentlemen?

The Ormistons' elderly retainer was both observant and articulate. Yes, he'd changed the wheel for the gentleman with the Princess staying up to Whitesisters, while he'd gone out in the Ford. No nail nor nothing, so it must have been one of those slow punctures. Maybe a leaking valve. The gentleman said he'd stop off at a garage on the way home, and have it seen to. The spare only wanted a bit of air. Very nice car, it was. Pity it had taken a nasty knock on the side. In a car park, the gentleman said, and no chance of finding out who'd done it. Yes, a real nice car. Jim Doubleday's grandson who worked in a garage in Crockmouth said that model had a Rolls-Royce engine. Gentleman had given him a quid for his trouble, which was a bit of all right, too.

Ignoring this premature hint, Pollard asked the old man if he had seen Mr Corden again.

Yes, he had, when he'd come off work Thursday evening. Five o'clock was knocking-off time. The gentleman had driven off a minute or two before, but when he, Jim Doubleday, came along on his bike, the car was drawn up by the hedge, a bit past the gates, and the gentleman was looking out his road on a map, with a pencil in his hand, and had given him a wave.

A couple of coins changed hands, and after thanking Jim Doubleday, Pollard told Toye to carry on.

'The details about Corden's car ought to have come in by the time we get back', he said, lighting a cigarette. 'It could mean running up to Town and getting a warrant.'

He expelled a mouthful of smoke, feeling both relaxed and exhilarated. This was it—this first real sighting of your quarry. It cancelled out all the waiting and worry and grind. His excitement mounted as the miles fled behind the car, the distant rumble of thunder and intermittent flashes of lightning assuming the character of an overture to a high-powered performance. As they came into Crockmouth the windscreen was suddenly spattered with gold as big drops of rain refracted the lights of the town.

Pollard strode into the police station and was handed a typewritten slip. The Yard informed him that Mr Maurice Corden of Stately Homes Limited, and 11, Robertson Road, W.8, was the owner of a smoke-grey Austin Vanden Plas Princess, registration number 2AO 779Z. He had hardly finished reading it when he was hailed by Inspector Diplock, looking triumphant.

'A report's come in on that car, from the enquiry we got out this morning,' he said. 'It was reported stolen from a street in Fulminster last Thursday evening, while the owner, a Mr Corden, was having a meal in the town. There's been no news of it since.'

The words were barely out of his mouth when a simultaneous blinding flash and a deafening crash of thunder directly overhead were followed by a hiss of rain like a giant fire extinguisher, dowsing Pollard's newfound optimism. He swore so uninhibitedly that Inspector Diplock looked startled.

'Corden's our man, and the bastard's managed to get rid of the car,' he concluded. 'I'm getting on to the Yard. It's bloody well *got* to be found.'

He vanished in the direction of the telephone, leaving Toye to explain the latest developments to Inspector Diplock. Presently he returned, looking tense.

'That ought to have got them off the ground,' he said. 'Every force in the country's being alerted. What time was the car reported missing on Thursday?'

'A quarter to nine,' Inspector Diplock told him. 'According to Fulminster, Corden came in to the station, saying he'd left the car in St Edmund's Street, near the cathedral, at about ten to eight, and gone off to have a meal.'

'How long does it take to drive from Whitesisters to Fulminster?'

'Say an hour and a half, under normal conditions.'

'Corden left Whitesisters at just on five. He should have got to Fulminster by half-past six, then. That allows an hour and a quarter—assuming he's speaking the truth—for getting rid of the car. It's not long. Unless someone else was involved, which doesn't seem likely, it can't be far away.'

Assured that both Fulminster and Crockmouth had put extra men on the search, Pollard's thoughts reverted to Maurice Corden.

'The more circumstantial evidence we can line up the better,' he said. 'Where did he spend Tuesday night, after getting away from the sandpit?'

Inspector Diplock remarked that there was nothing unusual in a chap spending the night in his car in a lay-by, and that enquiries had better be made from patrols on duty.

'Don't you think it's more likely he'd have had something perfectly normal lined up, sir?' asked Toye. 'After all, if he was acting independently, he couldn't have expected to come on Peplow. He could have found out about that dinner at Fulminster, and fixed his break-in to fit in with Lord Seton and Mrs Tirle being off the premises. Then he'd have gone on to an hotel somewhere in the ordinary way, with the miniatures in his luggage. Quite reasonable for him to spend the night in Crockmouth, seeing he was due at Whitesisters next day. He said he'd been making enquiries about the place on Wednesday morning, before going over there.'

'You've got something there,' Pollard said. 'A damn good point. What are the most likely hotels?'

Inspector Diplock made various suggestions.

'Thanks,' said Pollard. 'Let's go and try our luck, Toye. Better than hanging around doing nothing. We've had enough of that lately.'

It was deluging with rain. Turning up their coat collars they ran for the car. The shining streets were almost deserted. After several damp and profitless sorties they arrived at the Golden Bay, the Magnificent's rival. Here the manager was a youngish man, with an eye to some valuable free publicity for his hotel.

'I'll take you along to the night porter,' he said. 'It'll be the same chap who was on last Tuesday. There's a good bit of coming and going at this time of year, but he might remember anyone clocking in unusually late.'

The hotel register was produced, and showed that the last arrival on the Tuesday night of the previous week had been Maurice Corden, of 11, Robertson Road, W.8.

Pollard realised that he had been holding his breath.

'One up to you,' he remarked in an aside to Toye, and turned to the night porter, an elderly man who looked dependable.

'Can you remember what time this gentleman came in?' he asked.

'Few minutes after half-past twelve, sir,' the man replied without hesitation.

'How is it you're so sure?'

'I'd noticed from the list there'd been a room booked, and not taken up. Then we lock the front door at midnight. Guests wanting to come in after that has to ring. I remember I'd just gone to make meself a cuppa in the kitchen, an' had to switch off the kettle while I went along to the door.'

'Did Mr Corden arrive by car?' Pollard asked.

The porter looked at the register.

'Couldn't have, sir, or the car number'd be entered here. We always asks for it, in case the car has to be moved.'

'He could have missed out on that column, of course,' remarked the manager. 'I'll have some enquiries made in the morning, if you'll give me the number and a description. One of the maintenance chaps might have noticed it.'

'Thanks,' replied Pollard. 'That could be very useful. Can you remember what this Mr Corden looked like?' he asked the porter.

'Can't say I call him to mind very clearly, sir. There's so many in and out in the summer. Not old, he wasn't—in his forties, I'd say, with dark hair. I do remember that about him. Very pleasant-spoken gentleman. He said he'd had engine trouble on the way down from London, and that was why he was so late. I asked him if I could get him anything, but he said no, and I needn't trouble to show him up to his room, if I'd let him have the key. He'd only got a smallish case.'

'Did he seem excited or upset?'

'Not that I noticed, sir. A bit tired, I'd say.'

Feeling that there was no further information to be gained from the porter, Pollard thanked him, and moved away with the manager.

'Anything more we can do for you?' asked the latter.

'I'd like to know when the room was booked, and what time Corden cleared out on Wednesday morning.'

After a brief delay this information was forthcoming. The room had been booked some weeks earlier, from the Stately Homes office. After breakfasting in his room and paying his bill, Maurice Corden had apparently left the hotel on foot.

'He might have got the hall porter to whistle him up a taxi,' said the manager. 'I'll enquire into that too, if you like.'

Pollard thanked him again.

'I needn't urge complete discretion on anyone in your job, I know,' he added, with a grin.

'You're telling me! Haven't you noticed that I've asked no questions? I'm busting with curiosity, of course.'

'I'll go so far as to tell you that we're working on the Brent case, which I'm sure you know already. Also that it's possible that your pub may feature in the news one of these days.'

'Attaboy!' said the manager happily.

CHAPTER ELEVEN

POLLARD came down to breakfast the next morning with two alternative plans of action which he proceeded to put before Toye. The first assumed that there was still no news of the missing car. After ringing the owners of the other stately homes which had been robbed, to check on their contacts with Maurice Corden, they would attend the Peplow/Lambrooke funeral, and go on to Brent. Here they would try to discover, by indirect questioning of Lord Seton, if Corden was known to have had access to any of the Brent keys.

The second plan presupposed that news of the missing car suddenly came in. It could not even be formulated until the circumstances of the discovery were known.

As Pollard had expected, there was no news. Accordingly, at nine o'clock he settled down to a stint of telephoning, with Toye listening in and taking notes.

Admiral Miller of Great Loveridge House took the call himself. Hastily moving the receiver several inches from his ear, Pollard introduced himself and explained that the police were following up a fresh lead in the country house robberies, and were interested to know if the Admiral had ever considered opening his house to the public.

'M' wife did,' bellowed Admiral Miller. 'Dam' silly idea, too. Told her so from the start. Not enough here to attract people. We had a fellow down she'd heard of who called himself a consultant. Every Tom, Dick and Harry's a consultant or an executive these days. Charged a colossal fee, and then said just what I had.'

Asked for the consultant's name, the Admiral proceeded to

consult his wife. After some confused shouting he reported that neither of them could remember it, but the fellow's set-up had been called Stately Homes.

'What I want to know is when you chaps are going to get me my little Constable back. I wish to God I'd stepped up the insurance. Look at these picture sales at Sotheby's and Christie's . . .'

Massaging his ear, Pollard dialled Corridon Manor, and asked for the Honourable Mrs James Crabtree. After a lengthy delay an extremely U and rather elderly voice came over the line. Mrs Crabtree was delighted to hear that the police were still trying to find her little icons. They were great family treasures, apart from their value. They had been given to her great-grandfather when he was our ambassador at St Petersburg, by the Tsar himself.

Pollard made suitable comments, and brought the conversation round to the opening of Corridon Manor to the public.

'I see that you were advised by a firm called Heritage Houses,' he said. 'Did you by any chance consult any other in the first place?'

'I did, as a matter of fact.' Mrs Crabtree sounded surprised. 'I had been recommended to a Mr Corden of Stately Homes Limited. He came down here, and was very taken with the place. He went into everything thoroughly, and felt that there were distinct possibilities. Well, to be frank, I didn't take to him personally, or feel that we should see quite eye-to-eye about things, so I paid his initial fee, and then called in Heritage Houses.'

Pollard thanked her, and expressed the hope that the icons would soon be recovered.

Colonel Potter of Wyndhays Court was short. He failed to see how any idea he had entertained of opening the Court to the public could be relevant to the theft of his valuable collection of coins. Pollard was polite but insistent, and finally extracted the information that about two years previously the Colonel had been advised against opening

by a firm of consultants called Stately Homes. An insuffer-
able bounder had come down, called Cotton, or Cording or
some such name...

'Well, I suppose it's encouraging to have one's hunches
confirmed,' Pollard remarked, 'but the car's the thing. Get
ours round, will you, while I ring Brent and fix to see
Lord Seton after the funeral. We've got to get working on
these bloody keys.'

Crowds had gathered at the cemetery. In the chapel Pollard
and Toye slipped into seats in the back row kept for them
by Inspector Diplock. On running his eye over the crowded
pews Pollard was astonished to see Lord Seton and Robert
Tirle near the front. Was it the done thing, he wondered,
even if the chap found dead on your premises had come to
rob you? Or some atavistic assertion of the unadmitted
blood tie? Or a gesture of confidence, to cock a snook at
the police?

The arrival of the coffin under a mountain of flowers
distracted his attention. The little procession moved up
the aisle with George Snell as sole mourner. He watched
the congregation, but there were no reactions of interest
to him. After a time, however, it struck him that Robert
Tirle was very intent on the proceedings, and he began
speculating again. The young man could never have met
Lambrooke, of course... Was it remotely conceivable,
though, that the conversation in the maze had set him
thinking? If so, and he had worked things out for himself,
would youthful idealism lead him to speak out? And would
he have confided in that forceful young woman, the Lady
Caroline Tirle?

At the end of the short service the police officers went out
quickly to be present at the graveside. Here, too, a crowd
had collected. As George Snell stepped forward, prompted
by the undertaker, to scatter earth on the coffin, Press
cameras clicked busily. Everything was soon over, and
people turned their attention to the flowers.

162

'Where on earth did all these come from?' Pollard asked Inspector Diplock.

'Crazy women,' replied the Inspector. 'Except for Mr Snell's, that is. Look at this little lot.'

He pointed to a huge flamboyant sheaf. The attached card read 'To the Unknown, from Lonelyheart.'

Pollard shook off sudden distaste and compassion, and joined George Snell. As they walked back to their cars they discussed the legal position in relation to the dead man's estate. Finally George Snell got into his taxi and was driven away.

'Now for Brent,' Pollard said, getting in beside Toye.

Brent was showing signs of considerable activity. There were several cars standing in the forecourt, the great front door was open, and voices were audible. Pollard had to ring twice before anyone appeared. On stating his business he was hustled unceremoniously along the passage with Toye, in the direction of Peggy Blackmore's office. As they passed the hall Felicity Tirle's instructions to presumably newly-recruited guides could be heard. In the office Peggy Blackmore was regretfully informing someone that no more tea bookings could be taken for the following Saturday. She was dishevelled again today, but clearly from pressure of work, not anxiety.

'We're being simply *inundated*,' she assured Pollard, apologising for keeping him waiting. 'Yes, Lord Seton's back from the funeral. I'll tell him you're here.'

It's almost, he thought in astonishment, as though they've forgotten the whole affair ...

Lord Seton received them urbanely, with barely a trace of wariness in his eye.

'I'm afraid I've come with rather a long story,' Pollard said. 'In fact, with two interlocking stories. One of them starts so far back that it's most unlikely that we shall ever unravel its beginning. The other, we think, starts with the idea of opening Brent to the public, and this is where we're hoping you may be able to give us valuable information.'

Lord Seton regarded him impassively.

'May we go back,' Pollard continued, 'to the evening of Tuesday of last week? You, Lady Seton, and Mrs Giles Tirle were dining over at Fulminster. At about twenty minutes to ten a call came through on your private line. Mrs Pringle answered it, and a man's voice apologised for having dialled the wrong number. Immediately afterwards she heard the telephone ringing in Mrs Giles Tirle's house.'

Pollard went on to deal with the barking dogs, the Emmetts' admission of Dick White's visit, and the presence of the car in the sandpit which had scraped the van. He broke off the narrative to put in a plea for Bill Emmett.

'Silly chump,' Lord Seton said impatiently. 'The girl twists him round her little finger. He'd only got to ask if the boy could park—but I suppose he thought the stop-off might somehow leak out. What's all this leading to?'

'We now know who owns the car.'

Lord Seton looked puzzled.

'Well, what of it? There's no proof that the owner was involved in what happened here.'

'No direct proof at present,' Pollard agreed, 'but rather an odd thing has happened. He has reported that the car has been stolen. And in the meantime we have unearthed certain facts which suggest that he may have been involved in the earlier country house robberies.'

Lord Seton nodded abruptly.

'Sooner or later I felt sure this would come out.'

'Reverting to the alleged Peplow's death, the person who kicked him down those steps must either have been a resident of Brent or someone with the means of getting in— and out—without trace. If a resident, the field narrows to yourself, Emmett and possibly Mrs Giles Tirle. I don't think we need concern ourselves with Lady Seton, Mrs Pringle, or Mrs Emmett and her daughter.'

There was a fractional pause.

'Quite,' Lord Seton replied tranquilly. 'Naturally I

realised from the start that anyone with access to the public rooms that night was a potential suspect.'

'But,' said Pollard, 'what was completely out of character in each case was the ludicrous attempt to cover up what was almost certainly an accident. You and Mrs Tirle are far too intelligent and knowledgeable, and Emmett too simple.'

'A trifle backhanded, Superintendent, but I won't dispute the assessment.'

'We should, of course, have regarded the situation differently if any motive for the man's death could have been established.'

Pollard looked Lord Seton squarely in the face, and detected the faintest flicker of amusement. A silver cigarette box bearing the Tirle crest was pushed towards him.

'Thank you,' he said, helping himself, and passing the box on to Toye. 'To resume, if a resident wasn't involved, we had to look for an outsider. Our original idea—and I think yours—was that Peplow, as we'll still call him, had brought someone with him. We're now quite certain that the two men who were illegally in Brent that night had no connection whatever with each other.'

'Pretty incredible,' Lord Seton remarked, 'but presumably these million-to-one chances do come off sometimes.'

'They do. I can't give you details at the moment, but we are quite sure about it. As you know, Peplow came in as a visitor, gave his guide the slip, and made his way to the miniatures room without being spotted. He must, of course, have had previous knowledge of the house. The man who attacked him was almost certainly the one who made the wrong number telephone call. He knew about the dinner at Fulminster, and was checking up as a precaution. Let's call him X. It seems probable that he came in through your brother's part of the house, having the necessary keys. Our reconstruction is that he was examining the case containing the King Charles miniature, wearing rubber gloves, when Peplow heard him, started coming out, and threatened him with a gun. X kicked out in self-defence with unintentionally fatal results, slammed the panel shut—his prints are on it—and cleared off in a panic. He was further rattled by finding that a van had appeared in the sandpit, and he drove carelessly, scraping it as he went out.'

'If your reconstruction's correct,' Lord Seton said thoughtfully, 'X must have had both the key to my brother's place, and the one to the door leading into the public rooms. Only my sister-in-law has both these, apart from the emergency set in the safe. Are you suggesting that someone has managed to get at her key ring?'

'I think it's a possibility. Everyone puts down a key ring on a desk or a dressing table now and again, and in theory somebody with criminal leanings could have been around just then. But when we began thinking on these lines it struck us that there was a period when keys could have been at risk. I mean the time when Brent was being got ready for the opening. Weren't there workmen and others about who needed access to different parts of the house? One can picture keys circulating pretty freely at this stage.'

To Pollard's astonishment an expression of utter exasperation came over Lord Seton's face, not unmixed with triumph.

'I suggest you discuss this with my brother,' he said, reaching for the house telephone. 'Fortunately he got back from the States last night.'

Giles Tirle's study was in chaos. His desk was heaped with opened and un-opened mail, and coils of galley proofs. Every chair was piled with papers and books, and a suitcase half-full of typescript lay open in the middle of the floor. Robert Tirle, who had escorted his uncle and Pollard and Toye from the front door, began to clear a space for them to sit down.

Giles Tirle greeted the visitors with barely concealed annoyance. He was wearing a dilapidated pair of slacks and a faded shirt, his thick dark hair wildly ruffled, and he gave the impression of having been dragged out of intense preoccupation.

'Bit of a muddle in here,' he said shortly. 'My publisher's raising hell for these proofs. 'You'd better clear off, Robert.'

'Not on our account,' Pollard interposed. 'I'm sorry to disturb you, Mr Tirle. I merely want to ask you a few short questions. We're following up the possibility of skeleton keys having been used on the night a man was killed in the priest's hole. Lord Seton tells me you were in charge of work going on in the house during the August before the opening. How did the workmen get in and out?'

Giles Tirle stared at him frankly for a moment, as if trying to recall the events which had resulted in a police enquiry at Brent.

'Emmett—the caretaker—coped with all that sort of thing,' he said impatiently. 'We employed a reputable local firm that's worked for us for years. I strongly deprecate this tendency to go straight for the working man when a crime's committed—'

'For God's sake spare us your political bias,' Lord Seton interrupted. 'If you're not interested in getting this mess cleared up, the rest of us are.'

Pollard was conscious of Robert in the background, an unobtrusive figure leaning against the door.

'So you're quite sure, Mr Tirle,' he resumed, 'that you didn't personally hand over a set of keys to any of the men during this time? Or to anyone else?'

'Certainly not to any workman. I let Corden have the set, naturally, when he was down here drawing up the guidebook.'

'You mean that you let Corden have the emergency set of every dam' key in the place, for which you were personally responsible?' Lord Seton demanded in tones of ice.

'Don't talk like a bloody schoolmaster,' exploded Giles Tirle. 'Here I was sweating my guts out trying to arrange the rooms accurately, and get the Tudor kitchen reconditioned after it had been allowed to go to rack and ruin.

How the hell could I keep breaking off to unlock rooms and showcases for Corden?'

'It strikes me that the reconditioning of the kitchen raises an interesting point,' Robert remarked.

They all turned to look at him.

'What the devil d'you mean?' demanded his father.

'Well, after the walls were treated for damp, you had them replastered, didn't you? And the chaps who did it covered over the small ventilation holes belonging to the hole? I've wondered why on earth the bloke who was killed came blundering out, just asking to be copped. If he heard a noise in the room, you'd think he'd have lain doggo. Partly sozzled, perhaps, but my theory is that he hadn't realised there was no ventilation, and was dopey from lack of oxygen.'

'Are these priest's holes usually ventilated from outside?' Pollard asked.

'Frequently,' Giles Tirle began eagerly, in the confident tones of an expert. 'Quite often they led off chimneys, so—'

'So,' his son took up, 'the chap probably took an air supply for granted. He might have read up our hole. There are a couple of pages on it in a fairly well-known book on the subject of priest's holes. Or, of course, he might have been in ours before the kitchen was done up.'

There was a silence. Pollard observed that Robert Tirle was looking fixedly at his uncle.

'As the house wasn't open to the public before the re-plastering was done, that hardly seems likely,' Lord Seton replied coolly. 'Well, Superintendent, if my brother has given you the information you require . . .?'

'The area of the UK,' remarked the Assistant Commissioner, who had a penchant for statistics, 'is 88,745 square miles. Say a tenth of this is the maximum area in which Corden could have cached his car, assuming, of course, that he wasn't able to hand it over to a mobile pal. Roughly 8,874 square miles. Think of the available cover. Still, there are a lot of people around in the south of England at this time of year. Are you still dead against a broadcast appeal for information?'

'I don't want Corden to slip through our fingers, sir,' Pollard replied, not very happily. 'He must know that the car is bound to turn up in the end, and have got his escape route—or routes—open. I'd rather not precipitate matters until we've got our hands on the car.'

'Fair enough, as long as you're fully aware of the risk you're taking. It's up to you. There'll be a black mark against us for supposedly not having solved the identity riddle, of course. I've been taking soundings, by the way, and I think sleeping dogs will be let lie, provided we can establish whodunit. What's your next move? I don't imagine you'll be content to sit on your bottom until the car turns up?'

'No, sir,' Pollard replied. 'I feel the time's come to concentrate on Corden—as a person, I mean. You'll remember I've only seen him once, for about ten minutes, when he was talking to Lord Seton the whole time. Assuming that he committed these four robberies, and attempted the one at Brent, he's plunged in up to the neck. There may be further thefts, which haven't come to light. Nor has any of the loot. I want to find out what the motive is behind it all, and how he plans to cash in on the stuff. A chap who's got so many tracks to cover must be pretty well stretched, and might very well give himself away in conversation, for instance. I've been working out a plausible pretext for calling on him.'

'Any theory about motive?'

'Corden's a blatant social climber, sir. I got the impression that he'd sell his soul to get a footing in the landed gentry class. It could be that he wants cash to pull it off. He's doing quite well professionally, but I shouldn't think he's got capital.'

The A.C. grunted rather dubiously.

'I'm having him shadowed from the time I contact him,

sir,' added Pollard, interpreting the sound.

'Well, as I said before, it's up to you. By the way, I've picked up another interesting bit of gossip from my brother —the one who was up at Oxford with Lambrooke. Lambrooke had a girl-friend, and rumour went round that they were secretly engaged. I expect you can put a name to her?'

'Good Lord!' Pollard exclaimed involuntarily. 'Mrs Giles Tirle! So she *was* up at the time.'

'That's it. Somerville. Felicity Openshaw then, according to your file. Intriguing, isn't it? If she recognised Lambrooke last week, she must have had the hell of a shock.'

'If she did,' said Pollard thoughtfully, 'it could explain why no door was found open on the morning after Lambrooke was killed. She might have locked up after Corden, imagining that Lambrooke had been in the house during the night, and gone off again. Her one aim would have been to remove all traces of the visit.'

'That makes sense,' agreed the A.C. 'It's a fascinating case, Pollard. Sorry if you're finding it heavy going. Do you know what particularly appeals to me about it?'

'No, sir.'

'The thought of the Commissioners of Inland Revenue being done out of a round of death duties.'

Pollard went out with a grin which faded abruptly at the prospect of the immediate future. He found Sergeant Longman waiting for him with Toye. Longman had been doing a reconnaissance in Robertson Road. He reported pricey houses of an old-fashioned sort, which had been tarted up and turned into flats.

'Corden's got the first floor of Number 11,' he reported. 'The people below are on holiday in Majorca till the end of next week. I got that from the milkman. There's an old lady and her companion on the top floor. A fire escape runs down the back of the house into a yard. No garage. Corden garages in Morley Mews, round the corner, He's hiring a black Austin 1100 till he gets his own car back, he's given out, according to a chauffeur chap I chatted up.

Baker's just gone along to keep the house under observation, and Laxton will join him when he's followed Corden back from the office.'

'Always assuming he goes home from the office. Is Croot outside the office with Laxton by now?'

'Yes, sir, with a car at the ready.'

'Fine,' said Pollard. 'You've done dam' well, Longman. Now then, I'm going to take a calculated risk, and ring Corden.'

His call was put through with surprisingly little delay.

'You probably won't remember my name, Mr Corden,' he said pleasantly. 'We met very briefly at Brent last week. Detective-Superintendent Pollard. I'm ringing to ask you if you could manage to spare me a few minutes later this evening. This is quite off the record, but I've been trying to get some information about security at Brent during the pre-opening period from Mr Giles Tirle, and found it a bit difficult to pin him down. He happened to mention that you were working with him at one stage, so I thought I'd try you.'

A gust of laughter came over the line. Pollard found himself visualising Maurice Corden's dark head thrown back.

'I remember you all right. It was the morning after they'd found their corpse in the priest's hole, wasn't it? I'd dashed over from the Ormistons' place to try and buck up poor old Roger Seton. My God, you're telling me about Brother Giles! Can you imagine yourself trying to draw up the Brent guide book with him against time? Would you care to drop in on me this evening? I've got to take work home from the office, worse luck. It's 11, Robertson Road, W.8. Start bearing left from Kensington Church Street.'

Pollard thanked him, promised not to take up a lot of time, and rang off after arranging to call at about nine.

'So far, so good, I rather think,' he said. 'Now then, have we got everything taped? We leave here at half-past eight.

I drop you both off near the place, and arrive alone. Let's hope there's somewhere reasonably near to park. I go in, and chat with Corden for about fifteen minutes. Then you two come along, and ring his bell. Hold him as long as you can. For one thing, I've got a hunch that the loot is in his flat, and want to see what security measures he's taken. Even a couple of minutes would be better than nothing. Have you thought up anything yet?'

'We're local residents about informed rumours that the Ministry of Transport's planning to use Robertson Road as a diversion route for heavy lorries,' Longman told him. 'We're getting up a petition. Almost anyone in a posh area rises to that one.'

'It's an idea. OK, then. Zero hour's eight-thirty.'

When Toye and Longman had gone, Pollard tried to concentrate on arrears of work unconnected with the Brent case, but without much success. He was worried and depressed by the continuing failure to find Maurice Corden's car. It really seemed incredible that an Austin Princess could apparently vanish into thin air in a well-populated area of southern England. There was the feeling, too, of being up against a man possessed of an extremely competent brain, and unusual resource and coolness. And the whole case had had an elusive quality from the word go . . .

As always, however, when the moment for action arrived he was able to shake off his anxieties, and live only in the present. Reports had come in to say that Maurice Corden had left the Stately Homes office at his usual time, and driven himself home, discreetly followed by Croot and Laxton in a police car. He had shown no sign of going out again. Punctually at half-past eight Pollard started off with Toye and Longman. In the roaring tide of traffic at Hyde Park Corner the excitement of the chase suddenly returned to him. They made good time, and Toye, an excellent driver, unhesitatingly navigated a succession of side roads beyond Kensington Church Street. As they turned into Robertson Road he slowed, and late Victorian houses with an air of prosperity began to glide past.

'This'll do,' Pollard said. 'We won't risk being seen together. When I come out, I'll drive down to the far end and pick you up just round the corner. If there's no answer when you come to knock up Corden, take what steps you think advisable,' he added with a grin.

'We'll be around,' Toye said doggedly. 'Not so as anyone'd notice.'

They all three synchronised their watches, and Pollard took over the car. He cruised gently down the road, and manoeuvred into a vacant space just past Number 11. Looking up, he saw lights in the first-floor windows. A short length of path brought him to the front door. He rang a bell under Maurice Corden's name in a neat brass slot, and waited.

Almost at once quick steps sounded on the stairs, and the door was flung open.

'Superintendent Pollard? Good show. Found a parking lot? Oh, fine. No meters here yet, thank God. Come along up.'

The flats were pricey, all right, Pollard thought as he followed. Haircord carpet on the stairs. Fresh white walls and adequate lighting. No concrete and dank smells here.

The room into which he was led was unexpected. A wide archway had been cut in the wall originally separating front and back bedrooms. The result was a pleasing spaciousness. Pollard quickly registered modern basic furniture of good design, and a selection of attractive Victoriana softening the general effect with small intimate touches. There were good watercolours in gilt frames, and charming china figures on wall brackets.

It was a useful opening to the interview. Maurice Corden was gratified by his interest.

'Of course, anything remotely central and architecturally tops is utterly prohibitive,' he explained. 'So I decided to plump for something sound and turn-of-the-century, and then try to infuse just the right degree of restrained vitality into the excessive decorum. What will you drink? Or not?'

'Not, I'm afraid,' replied Pollard, 'but please don't be deterred yourself, will you?'

While a drink was being mixed he concentrated with all his powers on the room and its contents. Through the archway he could see an outsize kneehole desk under the far window. An anglepoise lamp directed a widening shaft of light on scattered papers. There were bookcases in both sections of the room, some containing obvious reference books. The one nearest to him held modern novels, paperbacks, and an old A.A. book in its vivid yellow cover. Various newspapers and periodicals, including *Country Life*, lay on a small table.

Maurice Corden came and sat down facing him, glass in hand.

'Smoke at least, won't you?' he said, holding out a cigarette box. 'What can I possibly do for you? Naturally I'm consumed with curiosity about the whole extraordinary business, being so involved with gorgeous, gorgeous Brent.'

Pollard crossed his legs, and hoped that he appeared relaxed.

'Then you'll have followed the case in the Press,' he said. 'Considering the melodramatic start, the reporting's been pretty sound, on the whole. Of course, it's been obvious from the start that two chaps were involved, Peplow, and the one who did him.'

Maurice Corden contrived to raise his glass with an astonishingly sardonic gesture.

'Cheers!' he said. 'Do go on.'

Pollard talked easily, giving nothing away, and closely observing the other as he did so. An interesting, but decidedly not a pleasing face, he thought. The eyes were slightly hooded, the nose too exploratory, the lips too thin. The lounging body in plum-coloured slacks, pale green shirt and black leather sandals of extravagant design somehow contrived to suggest calculation. Yet one could sense a latent nervous excitability.

'I'm afraid I'm in Lord Seton's bad books for making endless enquiries re security and keys,' Pollard said, raising a humorous eyebrow, a gesture at once reciprocated by Maurice Corden. 'There's no suggestion of casualness at the present time, but we've been thinking that there were probably a good many people around during the period when the house was being got ready for the opening. I gather quite a lot had to be done. When I heard that Mr Giles Tirle had been largely responsible for the various alterations, I went along to see him, the result being that I'm still thinking on the same lines, only more so.'

'My God,' said Maurice Corden with feeling. 'I only wish you could have been there to see it all. Brother Giles is probably the greatest contemporary authority on English domestic architecture and interiors, but he's also a single-minded excitable enthusiast, quite madly perfectionist where his shop goes. In all other departments of life he's utterly woolly and vague, and leaves everything to that terrifyingly competent wife of his. Once he got the bit between his teeth over opening Brent, there was simply no holding him. Roger Seton, who's a businessman, as you've doubtless realised, soon saw that if the place was ever to open at all, something had got to be done. He came to see me at the office, and we talked it over, and in the end I agreed to go down in August, when the rest of them were seizing their last chance of a family holiday in Scotland. I had the hell of a time, I can tell you.'

'I can believe that Mr Giles Tirle wouldn't be the ideal colleague if you were working against time,' Pollard remarked.

'Sure you won't change your mind?' Maurice Corden asked, getting up to fetch himself another drink. 'Well, somehow I got the furniture and pictures merry-go-round stopped, so that the guide book could be drafted, and then thankfully handed over to Roger Seton, who cut his holiday short.'

'He must have been exceedingly grateful. With all this

175

shunting round of stuff, I suppose keys were often in circulation?'

'Continually. There was redecorating going on, too. And it wasn't only a question of humping furniture and pictures. Giles had got a sort of general post of the contents of the showcases in progress as well. He was supposed to lock and unlock everything himself—there's some very valuable stuff at Brent, you know—but it certainly didn't work out that way. In fact, he swore like a trooper at anyone who interrupted him, chucked the keys at them, and told them to get on with whatever it was.'

'Were the various sets of keys on different rings?' Pollard asked, trying to spin out the conversation. Surely Toye and Longman would be along soon?

'Some were on rings with labels. The room keys—damn! Who on earth's that at the door? Sorry—I won't be a minute.'

Pollard moved swiftly into the other part of the room. The windows giving on to the fire escape were closed, and fitted with efficient safety locks. The door leading on to the landing had not been bricked up, but had a burglar-proof lock, and a stout bolt on the inside. A corpulent green baize draught excluder had been provided. Pollard prodded it with a sudden flash of excitement. It was rigid and heavy, but there was no time to investigate further now. Returning to where they had been sitting, he could hear voices actively engaged in conversation. The chaps were doing their stuff all right, but at any moment Corden could be back. He stood running his eyes systematically round the room. They lighted on a pile of Ordnance Survey maps on the bottom shelf of the bookcase.

He was on his knees in a flash. They were hellishly slippery things ... Taunton and Lyme Regis ... Bude ... Lancaster and Kendal . . . Salisbury . . . the conversation downstairs had an unmistakably penultimate note ... The Dukeries.

He found what he was looking for at the bottom of the

176

pile. As the front door shut, he was sitting in his chair with the Crockmouth and Fulminster sheets in his coat pocket.

'Can you believe it?' Maurice Corden demanded as he came into the room. 'That was a couple of chaps from further down the road. They've heard on good authority that the blasted Ministry of Transport's planning to divert heavy lorries along here.'

Pollard listened, commiserated, agreed that a petition was well worth while. Presently the conversation reverted to Brent. According to Maurice Corden keys had passed freely from hand to hand, including his own, he added with a laugh.

'Old Giles knows his stuff for sure, and he's a decent sort. Doesn't look down his nose at you, anyway. But I must say I got thoroughly fed up with him. If he'd had to make his own way like me, he dam' well couldn't have afforded this vague scholar-artist line. All right if you're born in the purple. Eton and Oxford—the whole bloody lot chucked in your lap.'

Pollard made an assenting noise and waited. He looked up to find Maurice Corden looking at him with an expression of such vindictive malice that he experienced a momentary shock.

'I suppose the obvious explanation's inadmissible, the precious Tirles being who they are?'

'Sorry?' Pollard replied. 'I'm not with you.'

'For heaven's sake! Of course you can't be, officially, but between these four walls . . . It's simple enough, surely? Peplow was a dam' fool of an amateur, who hadn't even got the sense to keep off the drink while he was on the job. He knocked back a flask of whisky, got fuddled, and came out like a lumbering elephant, making such a row that somebody heard and came along to see what was up. There was a scrap, in the course of which he went over backwards and fractured his skull. Whoever landed him the kick decided that the best thing was to shut the panel on him, and know nothing about it. Only as somebody happens to be thought blue-blooded, you people have to dish up a lot of tripe about a second chap having been in on the job, and ending up by bashing Peplow.'

'Who have you cast for somebody?' asked Pollard. 'Lord Seton?'

'Seton?' Maurice Corden almost shouted. 'Good God, no! Can you see that suave hard-boiled little tycoon losing his head like that? I mean that damned awful woman, Giles's wife. Surely it sticks out a mile? Don't you know she was in the Resistance in Occupied France? Decorated, what's more. Why don't you ask her how many Germans she shot, or knifed, or blew up? But she's a woman, for all that, and out of practice after all this time. Hence the panic.'

'If you've been a licensed killer, like a soldier or a Resistance fighter,' Pollard observed, 'I don't think you'd ever get out of practice, you know, either technically or psychologically. Just as you never forget how to swim or ride a bike, even if you haven't done it for years. To my mind this is the main objection to your reconstruction, which we've gone into pretty thoroughly, by the way. But there's a touch of the Amazon about the lady, I grant you.'

'If ever there was a bitch ... You should have heard her baiting me. Didn't think I was good enough to sit at table with them, I suppose. Arminel Tirle treated me like dirt, too, but at least she belongs to the set-up. The other one's no more blue-blooded than I am.'

Pollard wondered if he had ever heard a more psychologically revealing remark.

'Well,' he said, deciding to bring down the temperature, 'with all its snags you've created an extremely interesting job for yourself, and a much more pleasant one than mine. You actually founded Stately Homes, didn't you?'

Maurice suddenly reverted to good humour.

'Positively my own brain child,' he replied. 'I saw the possibilities when the Opening racket was getting under way in the fifties. I borrowed some cash and plunged in at the deep end. There's some competition now, but things aren't going too badly with the enormous development of coach tours taking people to see places. It's an incentive to owners to open. One day I'll be doing it myself, with any luck. Get hold of a small period place that's been let go to seed, and restore it. My God, don't I know the ropes! All I want's the necessary capital.'

He spoke with a kind of fierce determination. Pollard showed intelligent interest, and let the conversation run on. At last he glanced at his watch.

'I'd no idea it was so late. Too bad when you've got work on hand.'

'Not to worry,' Maurice Corden said, as they stood up. 'But I wish you people would find my car. Hiring's blue ruin, and I can't get a penny out of my insurance company at this stage. I simply must have a car. I've got to vet a place in Sussex this week, and another on the Welsh border the week after.'

For sheer audacity . . . Pollard thought, following him downstairs. He must have got everything absolutely sewn up. It was a disturbing thought.

A few minutes later he turned the car into the main road, and two figures emerged from the shadows.

'The Yard, and step on it,' he said, heaving himself across to the passenger seat. 'We may be on to something. Toye, do you remember that old boy Doubleday saying that he'd seen Corden sitting in his car on the Thursday evening soon after five, marking something on a map? It's a longish shot, but I managed to nick the Crockmouth and Fulminster Ordnance sheets when you chaps were chatting up Corden just now. It's remotely possible that we've got a lead.'

On their arrival in Pollard's room at the Yard the Crockmouth sheet was hastily spread out under a strong light. Bending over it, Pollard and Toye exclaimed in chorus. A rough dark circle, sketched in with a certain panache, was centred on Whitesisters.

Pollard brought down his hand with a crash on the top

of the desk.

'Those mouldering outbuildings behind Whitesisters! Old Ormiston said they only used one or two of them. In that set-up months could go by without anyone going into the others.'

'It'd be taking a colossal risk,' objected Toye, looking incredulous.

Pollard slumped down on a chair.

'Would it, though? Let's try to work things out. One's got to keep on remembering that if only Peplow hadn't hit on that particular night for his stunt, Corden's little game at Brent would probably have gone according to plan. Another Stately Home robbery, and what the hell are the police doing? But having killed Peplow—almost certainly accidentally—he suddenly finds himself up to the neck in a hideous crisis, which he makes worse by getting rattled and biffing the Crunchaway van as he drives out of the sandpit. He now realises that the damage to his own car could be circumstantial evidence against him, and decides that somehow or other he's got to get rid of it. He's anything but a fool, and soon sees that his best chance is to claim that it has been stolen. When it eventually turns up, he can swear that the damage has been done by the thief.'

Toye and Longman, following with rapt attention, made assenting noises.

'Well, then,' Pollard went on, 'having a plan of action steadies him. He also sees that the danger of being linked up with the van is greatest in the Brent-Crockmouth area, and that it will be safer to "lose" it on the way back to London. In the meantime, the less he's seen around in it, the better. Do you get me?'

'So he dumps it overnight in a big free car park, instead of turning up in it at the hotel?' contributed Toye.

'I think so. He's got to risk driving out to Whitesisters in it the next day, but when he gets there he has an unexpected run of luck. First of all, the people themselves—elderly and unsuspicious. Then the lie of the land and the garage he's given, which help to hide the scraped side of the car. Then that rabbit warren of derelict outbuildings which he explores perfectly legitimately in the course of his survey. It strikes him that here is a perfect hiding-place for the car, with a sporting chance of its not being discovered for months.'

'With any reasonable luck, giving him time to make his getaway?' asked Longman.

'This is it. He realises that when it is found, it will obviously be a pointer to himself, but by then he will have unobtrusively faded out while on a holiday abroad, having taken the best of his handy small-stuff loot with him. I'm quite sure he'll have had this part of the programme arranged all along. That's why I'm edgy about him at the moment. He's a clever devil.'

'The chaps are sticking around like limpets, sir,' Longman reassured Pollard. 'He won't slip through.'

'Let's hope you're right. What's biting you, Toye?'

'How did Corden get the car into one of these outbuildings without being spotted, sir? We know he left the place—Doubleday saw him—and to get back he'd have to drive right round the front of the house.'

'You've forgotten one small but vital fact, old son. The Ormistons were going out to drinks at some place on the far side of Crockmouth, and were due there at six. This would have come out in conversation when Corden's visit to Brent on Thursday morning, and the temporary hold-up in his survey of Whitesisters, were discussed, perhaps at breakfast on Thursday. Corden would have been reasonably sure that Doubleday would knock off at about five, and that the place would be empty. So he reshaped his original idea of abandoning his car on the way to London, and worked out the shortest possible circular route which would bring him back to the deserted Whitesisters. Let's have a look at it.'

They all three followed the marked route eagerly. It turned right off the valley road beyond Steepleford, crossed the ridge, bore right for a short distance along the coast road, and turned right once more, recrossing the ridge by a very minor road which rejoined the valley immediately above Whitesisters.

'What about the time factor, though?' asked Toye.

'He could have cut back across the ridge,' Pollard said, still staring at the map. 'It's barely a mile—less, if he took the footpath through the woods. There's a good bus service along that coast road between Crockmouth and Wythe Bay, and between Crockmouth and Fulminster. We've only Corden's word for it that he was in Fulminster by ten to eight. He didn't report the missing car to the Fulminster police till a quarter to nine.'

'Could have pinched a car in Crockmouth,' Longman suggested.

'Anyway,' Pollard said, reaching for the telephone, 'we'd better leave the details till we've actually landed the car . . . Get me the Crockmouth police station, will you? Priority.'

After some delay Superintendent Perry was forthcoming.

'Sorry to rout you out at this hour, Super,' Pollard said, 'but I think we know where Corden's car is.'

The Super was gruffly congratulatory, concealing obvious disappointment that his own men had failed to bring off the coup.

'You'll handle the next stage at your end, won't you?' Pollard said. 'Go along and search the place, and take possession of the car, always assuming it's there. Then ring us from the house, if you will.'

'OK. First thing tomorrow do? Bit late for tonight, isn't it? You say you've got Corden covered?'

It was finally settled that the search party should arrive at Whitesisters by eight o'clock on the following morning.

'We'd better make tracks for home and a few hours' sleep,' Pollard said as he rang off. 'Tomorrow could be quite a day.'

Heading for Wimbledon through the blessedly empty streets, he experienced a feeling of anticlimax. After all, even the car was to some extent purely circumstantial evidence. Wouldn't Corden have gone to all possible lengths to remove every possible trace of the van's paintwork from the scraped area? There mightn't be enough left for the forensic chaps to get a decisive result. And he would have done that last drive in gloves. The defence could argue, even if implausibly, that a car thief could have known about the Whitesisters outbuildings. Even if all the stolen property were recovered, it wouldn't clear up the Brent case.

Pollard's mind went back uneasily to Corden's remark about going down to Sussex to see a potential client. For Sussex, read Gatwick, he thought. Could a flight have been booked under an assumed name, Corden having managed to get a forged passport? Airports and ports had better be alerted, he decided, as he turned into his road.

He let himself into the house noiselessly, and crept upstairs. Jane roused, but only momentarily as he slipped into bed. He kissed the top of her head, and lay staring at the curtains as they swung gently against the faintly luminous windows. He felt teased by kaleidoscopic uncertainty. If only Corden could be startled into betraying himself about Brent . . .

Astonishingly it was daylight, and there was emptiness at his side. As he sat up in bed Jane came in, Andrew, wide awake and perky, on her arm.

'Coffee's ready when you are,' she told him. 'I had a hunch that you'd want to be off early.'

By a quarter to eight he was at his desk, having dealt with the alerting of airport and port authorities. In front of him lay the warrant for Corden's arrest, and another authorising a search of the flat. A report had come in that no attempt had been made to leave the flat during the night. Toye and Longman arrived together, and Pollard began to discuss alternative courses of action. If the car turned up at Whitesisters, the first essential would be to send down a forensic expert. Then—

The burr of the telephone cut in.

'Crockmouth,' he told the other two. 'Ahead of schedule. Couldn't wait to get out there, I suppose.'

There were a few seconds of tense waiting, and Superintendent Perry came through.

'Hand it to you!' he bellowed, in a voice clearly audible to Toye and Longman. 'It was stowed away in a tumbledown outhouse full of junk and cobwebs. Where do you want us to go from here?'

There was a brief jubilant exchange, and discussion of safeguards until the Yard expert could get down. Then Pollard rang off, and immediately put through a request for assistance to the Forensic Department.

'Someone'll be along right away,' he said. 'Now, then, what we've got—'

He was interrupted once again by a report from the car shadowing Maurice Corden's movements. Corden had left Robertson Road in his hired Austin, and was heading eastwards, as if making for his office. A suitcase and a briefcase had been brought from the flat and put into the car.

'OK,' said Pollard. 'Over.'

He turned again to Toye and Longman, but had barely begun to speak when the telephone rang. He snatched up the receiver impatiently. Watching him, they saw his face go suddenly tense as he barked a curt question. There was a brief exchange, and he slammed down the receiver.

'Stately Homes office,' he said, reaching for the two warrants, and making for the door. 'Perry's found out that while they were gooping at the car, that fool of an Ormiston woman rang the office and left a message for Corden, giving him the good news. We've got to beat him to it. Anything could happen.'

The journey had the genuine nightmare touch, Pollard thought, sitting rigid at Toye's side at the height of the morning rush hour. His ears strained for another radioed report of the Austin's progress, while his eyes were rivetted by the inhuman despotism of the traffic lights. The close-packed mass of cars produced a sensation of claustrophobia, and the calculated risks taken by Toye during the brief periods of mobility were frankly terrifying.

As they emerged on to the embankment, Corden was reported in a big traffic block on the west side of Piccadilly Circus.

'Bar accidents, we'll make it,' Toye muttered.

All the time, beneath his immediate preoccupations, Pollard found himself rehearsing the arrest. Properly handled it could—just conceivably—spark off a reaction that was an admission.

He was still undecided when he leapt out on to the pavement outside the Aldwych office block which housed Stately Homes Limited, on its fourth floor. Leaving Toye to enlist the help of a traffic warden over the parking of the car, he joined the stream of men and women passing through the doors into the entrance hall. After a hasty glance round he went across to make himself known to the startled porter at the Reception desk.

A minute or so later he returned to Longman and Toye, conscious of a longing for the business to be over.

'The porter says Corden's almost always in by nine,' he told them. 'We'll take him in the lift. It's less public than up in his office. The lift's self-operating, and the porter's going to divert anybody who tries to follow us in. You go in after Corden, Toye, keeping your face turned away, and your thumb on the ground floor button, for God's sake. Longman and I will come in after you.'

They waited, for what seemed an eternity, Pollard watching the entrance from behind a newspaper, Longman and Toye ostensibly reading the noticeboards. The flow of arrivals thinned to a mere trickle as the minute hand of the clock on the wall crept up to the hour in a series of jerks. At last Corden came briskly up the steps, swinging his briefcase.

Toye crossed the hall and brought down the lift. On its arrival he stepped inside, followed by Corden, Pollard and Longman. The latter shut the gates, and the three detectives faced inwards for the moment of recognition.

'Maurice Corden,' Pollard heard himself saying, slowly and deliberately, 'I hold a warrant for your arrest. I have to warn you that anything you say may be used in evidence. You are charged with—'

In the harsh, unshaded light of the lift cage Corden was white and sweating. He moistened his lips as Pollard spoke.

'It was an accident,' he broke in hoarsely. 'I swear it was.'

'You are charged,' Pollard resumed, keeping steadily on course, 'with the theft of property from Admiral Miller, of Great Loveridge House, the Honourable Mrs James Crabtree, of—'

With a shrill scream of fury Corden flung himself forward, to be seized and pinioned by Toye and Longman.

'You vile devil, you've tricked me ... But it was an accident, I tell you. I never meant to kill the fool. He came up out of that bloody hole like the dead in that ghastly thing in the church. He'd got a gun, I tell you ... I only meant to kick it out of his hand ...'

EPILOGUE

THE NEWS of Maurice Corden's arrest exploded in a blaze
of publicity. It was pre-eminently a story. In addition to
the sensational charges on which he was committed for
trial, there was the incomparable background of titled
families and stately homes. The unidentified victim found
in the romantic setting of a priest's hole was almost an
embarras de richesses.

Photographs of Brent blossomed in the papers and on
the nation's television screens. So, too, did those of the
other country houses which Corden was alleged to have
robbed, and even some of those to which he had merely
rendered his normal professional services. There were interviews with those of their owners and owners' employees
who could be prevailed upon to give them. Experts wrote
articles on the architecture and contents of the houses, one
of which started up a passionate correspondence in *The
Times* about the date of a famous refectory table at Wonbridge Castle, in which Giles Tirle took a heated part.

Pollard himself was accorded a measure of recognition
which surprised him.

'It's got its comic side,' he remarked to Jane, throwing
down an evening paper. 'Suppose they knew I'd unearthed
Lambrooke into the bargain?'

'That's all officially shelved, I take it?' she asked, holding
up and critically inspecting the frock she was smocking for
Rose.

'Yes. The A.C. sent for me this afternoon. They've had
a top-level hush-hush conference with the Director of
Public Prosecutions and others. It was agreed that as it's

a sheer impossibility to get conclusive evidence of the identity swop, or that any of the family recognised Lambrooke for sure, the only course is to let the whole thing drop.'

'Sensible,' Jane commented. 'Do you suppose there'll be an inspired leak to Lord Seton that the file is closed?'

'I wouldn't know. Such a matter would be much too exalted for a mere C.I.D. Super. Personally, I don't think it's necessary. I'm convinced that he worked it all out for himself almost from the word go, and isn't losing any sleep over it.'

'Did you see that they're extending the open season at Brent by a fortnight?' she asked.

'No!' exclaimed Pollard incredulously, retrieving the newspaper. 'Where was it?...Oh, I see...I must say I hand it to them.'

Lord Seton's insistence on cashing in on Brent's spell of phenomenal popularity had carried the day, in spite of strong opposition from Lady Arminel on the grounds of the excessive wear and tear to the lawns. The latter part of the summer was gruelling to all concerned, but highly remunerative, and effective in discouraging any inclination to dwell on the immediate past. It struck Pollard, however, that the family had shown a centrifugal tendency, once Brent had closed its doors. During a flying visit to Crockmouth in connection with the preparation of the case against Maurice Corden, he learnt from Inspector Diplock that Lord and Lady Seton were on a visit to British Columbia, and that Mrs Giles was with her French relatives. After having no end of returfing done, Lady Arminel was away on a golfing holiday at St Andrews, up in Scotland. They could all do with a break, in the Inspector's opinion, after the nasty time they'd had, and then the thousands of visitors on top of it all.

Pollard reflected that Giles and Robert Tirle would be back in Oxford for the start of the university term. He wondered briefly how Caroline was getting on at her secretarial college, and if she had gained her point about being a Third or Fourth Girl in a London flat.

Time slipped by, and the Brent case came on at the Old Bailey in November. Connoisseurs of crime were heard to remark that, for a case with such a spectacular beginning, the trial was disappointingly tame. Maurice Corden pleaded Not Guilty to the manslaughter charge, alleging that he had been threatened with a gun, and merely tried to kick it out of the deceased's hand. The fact that a revolver had been found in his flat, and identified by George Snell as the property of the deceased, carried considerable weight with the jury. They brought in a verdict of Guilty, but with extenuating circumstances, and the sentence was a relatively light one of three years. The temperature was further lowered by the accused's plea of Guilty to five charges of robbery, and one of attempted robbery at country houses where he had been employed. The defence made great play of the fact that he had voluntarily disclosed to the police the whereabouts of all the stolen property, all of which was being returned to its rightful owners. After some scarifying remarks about breach of trust, the judge passed a five-year sentence, to run concurrently with the other, and Maurice Corden duly disappeared from the public scene.

Pollard witnessed his exit with relief, and proceeded with the task of getting the recovered property identified by its owners, and duly handed over to them. Their reactions varied. Admiral Miller, in addition to an official letter of thanks, reciprocated with a brace of pheasants. Colonel Potter meticulously checked over his collection of coins at the Yard, signed a receipt, departed, and was heard of no more. The Hon. Mrs James Crabtree, who proved to be an old friend of the Assistant Commissioner's, issued an edict that Pollard should bring her icons to Corridon Manor in person, and take luncheon with her.

'You'll have to go, Pollard,' the A.C. told him. 'It's more than my life's worth to refuse. It'll be an experience for you: she's one of the few surviving *grandes dames*. You'll get a first-rate meal, and the place is a little gem.'

Contrary to his expectations, Pollard enjoyed his visit immensely. He found himself completely at home with the authoritative old lady, whose perceptive comments on Maurice Corden astonished him. After all, he reflected, she was the only one of all these people to shy off the chap in the first place . . .

As the A.C. had forecast, the lunch itself was admirable, and served by a butler of traditional type. Over coffee Pollard was exhaustively cross-examined on the subject of his family and home. He finally took his leave with a superb azalea from the Corridon greenhouses in the back of the car, a present for Jane.

A comfortable feeling of finality descended upon him as he drove away. At last the whole intricate worrying business had been satisfactorily wound up.

In the event, however, this conclusion was premature. On the following afternoon pale gold sunshine and a sparkle of frost on fallen leaves tempted him to make a brief detour in St James's Park. A young man and a girl, walking towards him hand-in-hand, were for a moment vaguely familiar figures, and then suddenly identified. During an exchange of greetings Pollard noticed that while Caroline Tirle remained jubilant, Robert had become poker-faced.

'Mr Pollard!' Caroline told him, 'we're publicly engaged! It'll be in *The Times* tomorrow. When he came down for the Christmas vac, Robert tackled Daddy again, without saying anything to me, and somehow got him round. I simply can't think how he's done it, after all the fuss. Aunt Felicity's caved in, too. When we went to tell her Daddy had given way, she looked at Robert, and then laughed and laughed. Mummy's never been against it, really, you know. She just thinks it's her duty to back up Daddy. Actually, I'm certain she's glad. Her daughter for Brent.

The family firm carries on, and all that.'

'No opposition from my father, of course,' Robert took up, his poise regained. 'His mind's above these little family matters. I always think my mother must have popped the question you know. Only Aunt Arminel remains implacable, but she'll come round in time: too practical to refuse to accept a *fait accompli*.'

Pollard listened fascinated to these accounts of the reactions of the Tirles, all so perfectly in character. He was warm in his congratulations, and enquired about future plans. The wedding was to be in the following autumn, he learnt.

'You'll have your First in the bag by then', he said to Robert. 'Have you fixed on your career yet?'

'Come to that, sir,' the young man replied, 'I've been toying with the idea of looking you up for a spot of advice. I've found this affair at Brent and its ramifications absorbing, you know. Are there any prospects in the C.I.D. for a chap like me?'

'Excellent ones,' Pollard told him. 'But I'd stick to the idea of going into the Diplomatic, if I were you. I can see a highly promising career for you there.'

Their eyes met squarely, and Robert Tirle gave him a broad grin.